Heavenly Realm Publishing
Houston, Texas

Unless otherwise indicated, all scriptures quotations
in this book are from the Holy Bible King James Version,
Amplified, and NIV version.

This book is solely the author's imagination. Names, places,
events are from the author's imagination and are not intended
to harm, copy, infringe, or reveal real life situations.

ISBN—13: 978-1-937911-39-3

Library of Congress Control Number: 2012939749

This book is printed on acid free paper.

Printed in the United States of America

Published By: Heavenly Realm Publishing
16760 Hedgecroft Dr., Suite 614
Houston, TX 77060
www.heavenlyrealmpublishing.com
 Toll Free 1-877-599-3237.

GOD *Loves Thugs* TOO!

AN URBAN, FICTION NOVEL
&
MYSTERY & ACTION PACKED

Stephanie Franklin

BOOKS BY STEPHANIE

1. When Ramona Got Her Groove Back from God
2. My Song of Solomon
3. My Song of Solomon *Prayer Journal*
4. Position Your Faith for Great Success
5. Position Your Faith for Great Success *Workbook*
6. The Purpose Chaser: For Children Ages 5 to 12
7. God Loves Thugs Too!

CONTENTS

THE MESSAGE

You as the reader, are in for a time of your life. *"God Loves Thugs Too"*, shows that God loves everybody and He can change anybody's life who allows Him to. He can change what seems like a defeated life, into a victorious life. What is dysfunctional, into a functional—rewarding life.

This fiction novel is meant to show that those who think God can only save only certain types of people are wrong. God can change anybody's life. He is no respect of persons. It shows that although we all come from different backgrounds, different lifestyles and have different testimonies, God can still save and change anybody's life. This novel shows some graphic writing, details, and writing style that may not be politically correct in order to show the imperfection of who Joe is and lifestyle he is living. It has to take you into his world in order for you to understand the atrocious life that he is living. So please do not judge, just hold on to your seat belt because you're in for a ride of your life...

THE REVIEW

Joe grew up in an infested project in the urban, ghetto of Bronx, New York with a prostituted crack-head mother and a father he never knew. He had to grow up fast, facing the fact of what people thought about what a thug is, and the fact of his mother being mentally challenged, and couldn't provide for him the way a wholesome mother could. From this experience, he became one of the largest drug lords, pushing crack cocaine, pimping women, and robbing every business that made them a prey to his quick in and out strip of their items. He knew how to play the cards, "get in quick and you won't get caught". They—he and his gangster crew, held on to this until things got out of hand and the only thing they had left was love, loyalty to the thug life, and the power of over-coming the law. Joe would do anything to stay on top until Pricilla—his one-and-only love, found a little soft spot in his heart, which was hidden by the hardness of what a thug is supposed to be, and how he is supposed to act. The fact that he doesn't believe in God, and the hidden inner fear of the fact that he later realizes that he does need Him, brings him back to the reality that he can't make it without Him.

THE PREVIEW

Where I grew up, it was violence and crime on one side and the fast lane of sexual prostitution on the other. You either get with it, or you get left out or blowed away. "Let me explain what my definition of what a thug is so that it can forever be broken down. Some people think that a thug is a low life—a person who ain't got no future, or all a thug thinks about is gettin' women; and smokin' weed in the hood. Thugs do love them some women, but they're not low life's. They do have a future. Each person is accountable for their own actions. My name is Joe, and I'm one of em'. I'm a thug at heart who runs the streets as a notorious gangsta'. I'm what you call the good, the bad, and the ugly. I come raw. I tell it like it t-i-is. I'll do anything to get my way. I'll even love you on the inside, but not on the outside cause' I don't wanna' break my thug image—which shows hardness at all times. The sex scenes in this book are not depicting that all thugs are sex feigns, just depicting that I'm a sex feign. I loves me some women, liquor, weed, and the urban—hustlin' thug life of sellin' dope and snifin' powder. A lotta' people get us thugs mistaken like we run from love, but we don't run from love, we actually run to love. But what we run from is the mistaken'. Cause' we always mistaken of somethin' and somebody. Mistaken of somethin' we accused of doin' and sayin', and mistaken of somebody we ain't never seen befo'—ain't never came

iii

into our presence. That's what has made me a mad dawg' in this world called society."

THE REMINISCE—97'

Her breath smells like rich honey. Her eyes are glowin' like a diamond in the dark. The darkness of her smooth chocolate cream colored skin is in competition with the hottest model on the Hollywood runway. I dig her long chocolate 5'9 frame with long coal black hair that's so freshly done. Kinda' got that executive look about her. She ain't no gangsta' type female—the ones I dig the most. Met her at the park with her female friends tryin' to play hard to get. I see it wasn't that hard. Got the invitation on the first call. She say she a Christian, which I disagree cause' she gave it up the first night I met her. That's why I'm back for more. Oops, forgot, I got her mixed up with this other female I met last week. But I think I can still get me some from this one too. She a tough lil' ol' cookie. Say she a Christian too. Probably like the other one, weak. She gotta' long, chocolate 5'9 frame too. Kinda' look like twins. They both got that executive look about em'. Can't even touch her without her first givin' me the, I'll knock you out eye. She somethin' else. Won't buldge even if I promise to put a condom on. I smirked at the thought. I likes me a challenge cause' I ain't never lost one.

She wouldn't let me see her body before she jumped under the covers while I was preparin' myself in the bathroom—wrappin' it up—my secret. I guess she don't want me to see her body. Which ain't no thang. I ain't got to see her body to get what I want. I went and jumped in the bed. She laid her head on my hairy chest. I see she like to tease a brotha'.

She took a slight breath, then whispered in my ear. "I'm so glad you came back to see me Joe."

"I'm glad I came back too, my sweet Candy." I whispered back with a tease hopin' that that'll work to get me some—NOT. The satin sheets slid across my lower waist, as my left hairy leg rubbed across the top of her thick slightly muscled toned thighs. I made my way on top. I'm not wearin' anything but she got the nerve to have these big ol' pajamas on; of course.

CR

The after math of her and my affection of a thirty minute 4-play made me cringe, cause' this sista' still won't give it up out of all the work I just did. There's nothin' I can say or do to get my way. Nothin'. Not even when I slightly blew my breath in her ear, whispered sweet words into her heart, rubbed on everything, she still won't give it up. One thing she did do was sighed at my touch and took a slight breath at my circular motions. But the brawd still won't give it up. This' a strong one.

She jumped up and yelled, "Get up!" like she just seen somethin'.

"What up?" I asked, poppin' up. She got me a little scared but I won't let her know it.

"You gotta' go, shouldn't have ever let you get me to this point. I love God too much to be actin' like I don't belong to Him!"

I jumped up and put my clothes on with an attitude and said, "what ever. Hey, I'm goin' to the store to get me some Swishers."

"Ok what ever." She said, slowly gettin' out of the bed and following me to the front door of her one bedroom and a tiny lil' bathroom town home.

"That's all you gon' say?" I had to ask.

"Yep." She stepped back from the door. "O' you gave me something to reminisce about when I think about getting married."

I looked at her crazy at first then smiled. "The reminisce huh'?" We both thought about it and smiled. "Man now I know you're a Christian." I said.

"I am now. See you later." She nudged me out of the door and closed it behind me makin' me think about what she just said.

I burnt off down the stairs feelin' like a sucka' who just lost a bet.

ଔ

After that night, I never saw Candy again. She was the first one who wouldn't give me my way. She wouldn't even let me see her body that I longed to see. At least I did get her in the bed, but nothin' happened to please my horizons and inner most desires. My imagination wasn't even enough. I'm still relyin' on my imagination. It's cool—that's the toughest chick I've ever met with a rap and a popularity to be reckoned with. On my end, I ain't never had no problem with gettin' no female. She was the first. She ain't nothin' to mess with.

THE INTERLUDE

Sirons sounded my eardrums like a horn player playin' in the badest band. I know they're close but not too close for comfort, I smirked. Pricilla—my fine lil' ol' gem. Her smile lights up my life. A thug could never admit that a chick could steal his heart cause' that would make em' soft. But I don't mind bein' soft for this star. I love to watch her on stage—my stage—right in front of my bed. Yea'! I thought, as I just had a flash back. A loud skid and a quick ka'-bomb brought my thoughts back to reality. I'm bein' chased by the police! It's the norm. They chase, but they don't catch. I jumped out of the crashed get-a-way SUV after crashing it into a lil' ol' Toyota on the side of the road, and now I'm runnin' into a high hay field thinkin' I can't get caught. The kinda' field I bet some ol' man takes good care of. The darkness is blindin' my eyes as I ran into nowhere. The fuzz is closing in on me fast, I oughta' give up but that would defeat the purpose of the chase. I likes me a good chase, makes the adrinalin' aroused. Their shouts of hate—"I'm gon' get you for makin' me chase you, you @^%$*%@!" "You'll never get away with what you've done, you %^@*$%!" I just heard somethin' that caught my ears: "Hey! Everybody stop, just let k-nine get em', he'll give up!" Somethin' about those words just made a

Gee knees get weak. I ran a little further when my imagination became a reality. All of a sudden a German Shepherd's claws clenched into the back of my leg, which ain't no joke. Another one gripped and locked into the back of my thigh, and the last of several gnawed and growled at their many bits. I can hear the fuzz laughin' at my shouts—as I shouted like a woman for help. Cross would die laughin'. "Get em' off of me, get em' off of me, please!" I screamed and yelled. Grass and dirt shoved into my mouth and nose as I scrambled to get away, but another German Shepherd opened up his mouth like a gator and caved into the back of my neck as he pushed my face into the dirt. Now I'm light headed and nauseated. I've lost a lot of blood. The pain is unbearable. "Man!" I yelled. "Get these @%#& dogs off me you @%#& fool!" I can feel the fuzz standin' over me lookin', laughin', and makin' smart remarks. Man, I'm wounded and I ain't got no pistel to fight back.

"You shouldn't have done what you did and this wouldn't be happenin' to you!" One of the fuzzes yelled like he the head man in charge. "Why did you run?" The dog launched at me and bite me again. "Huh'?"

The result of that bite made me answer. "I ain't got no answer, get these mut's off me!"

Inside I know I shouldn't have done what I did. A thug never tells his secrets—he just do what he gotta' do. SURVIVE.

I blacked out.

&

Hours have gone by in this freezin' police station. The fuzz have been terizin' me, askin' me why I did what I did. They ain't got no evidence, so my mouth is sealed. I'm still in the same chain with the same loud mouths yellin' in my ears talkin' bout' nothin'. Ain't gon' make me snitch, I don't care what they say. A thug never snitches, no matter what the case is.

CB

They finally gave up after five hours of interrogation. Like I said, they didn't have no evidence. I ditched the 22 in the gutter. Easy. I can't lie, I had to get em'. The nigga' should've paid me my cash. I don't play with my money. If he hadn't of ran his mouth, I wouldn't have popped em' so many times. He got what he deserve. They found em' just where I left em', in the alley right in the dumpster, cause' that's what he was—trash.

GOD *Loves Thugs* TOO!

AN URBAN, FICTION NOVEL
&
MYSTERY & ACTION PACKED

It's a cold chill December day in the heart of the winter, and I'm chillin' in my sparklin' silver Benzo in South Bronx. The boys is supposed to be meetin' me down by the alley where we all hang out. Tonight's gon' be a night to remember. The only problem I got is Pricilla. She ain't cuttin' a nigga' no slack. I can't take a breath without askin' her for permission. She's more controllin' than my crack head momma. I ain't gon' even talk about my Pops, I ain't never met him befo'. Probably in somebody's pen. One thing I do rememba' was what Moms was tellin' me about the fact that he claimed me, unlike the rest of the eleven kids he's supposed to have by her and somebody else. But she don't know where non' of em' at, except me. I'm the only one she didn't give away. All this info came when she was so-called sober.

Back to Ms. Pricilla, I care about her and thangs but I can't be havin' no woman that be tryin' to do my job. It's a man's job to over-power the woman, at least that's what I was always taught by watchin' my Mom's life. Men came and went out of her life like it wasn't nothin'. Some beat her unconscious, while others controlled her every move. I watched this, and always thought that that's what a man is supposed to do. But Ms. Pricilla ain't havin' that. If anything, I'm runnin' from her. I'll never tell my boys that though. I wanna' laugh, but I'm too embarrassed.

I'm a thug at heart. I was raised to be a thug. Most of the time I had to take care of my blowed out moms. I had to fight for the both of us. I got tired of gangsta' men beatin' on her, pimps beatin' down our raggedy one bedroom project penthouse lookin' for either their money or sex. I had to be a thug just to survive the hard life and the cold-hearted reality of the ghetto' life style which came at no surprise. On the outside, I'm a gangsta-fied—thick, 6'5, 280-pound, tattoo wearin', baldhead with goatee, sparklin' white cosmetics grill, charcoal chocolate lookin' brotha' with a milky way smile that would knock any female off her feet. But on the inside, I'm a scared lil' ol' chicken with a big ol' teddy bear heart that need a lot of love. I would give anybody my last til' they cross me wrong. I don't know why, but I have this burst of anger that only comes out when somebody say or do somethin' crazy to me, and because of this, I've secretly killed a total of about eighteen men and women. There ain't no discrimination with me specially when they try to check a brotha' the wrong way. Most of em' my boys took the wrap for, and the others they couldn't either find the murder weapon, or nobody ever snitched. In my opinion, I'm one of tha' most well known black thugs in the Bronx—so I think. I've been this way for goin' on 28 years—all my life. But somehow all this don't mean nothin' to me no more. I'm ready for a new life but I don't know how to come out of what I'm doin'. Can't tell nobody my true feelings cause' they wouldn't take me serious. Then they so selfish, thinkin' of their own needs, they wouldn't let me go. My boy Cross is one of em'. I can't dream too hard cause' one thing about it, once you in, you in. There's no comin' out. It would only take the Man Upstairs to change all this.

○8

Traffic is bumper to bumper slow. The sound of the horns reminds me of rush hour on the NYC busy streets. I can't stand traffic, makes me feel trapped. My boys say I'm claustrophobic, but I disagree, I'm just not a clingy dude. I take that back I am a clingy dude—only to my women. I laughed to myself. I mean to my woman Pricilla. I'm only clingy cause' she so fine and her looks are to kill. I always wanted an out goin', bright, not too smart cause' then she'll think she's smarted than me, a beautiful, fine, sexy, fine, sexy, fine, somethin' somethin' somethin' and what else do a brotha' need?—Nothin'. An all in one package. A person would think with all I got goin' on, I have a bright future ahead of me.

Pricilla, my street life, my hustle, my boys… somethin' else's supposed to be goin' on, I just can't put my finger on it.

&

As I pulled up in the projects in broad day light, some are out doin' their thang while hustlers are everywhere gettin' their hustle on; as the sun beamed down makin' our foreheads shine. Others are shootin' dice, standin' around with a bottle in one hand and a joint in the other, playin' basketball with the grocery basket hangin' from a broken light poll. Prostitutes are well on their job, o' by the way, got some of them too. I own about three of em'. I'm trin' to establish a corporation with em'. All three of em' do what ever I tell em' to do. I'm a rich brotha' and I don't have to do nothin' but sit up and collect. Pricilla used to be one of my call women til' she started taggin' a long with me, then I stopped her cause' I didn't want no disease nor did I want AIDs. I wanted to be the only one she's sleepin' with. Even though she's not the only one I'm sleepin' with.

My boys are where they supposed to be, in the alley between the projects. All five of em'. Only two of em' I really cut for. The rest of em' I'm just usin' to rob this liquor store down on Fifth Street. I'm just fickle like that. I'm subject to change on you in a minute. Plus I don't like rollin' in packs, to easy to be seen and plus that means less women for me. I know I don't need the money but its quick cash. We've robbed em' about twenty times and they ain't caught us yet. As long as we're in and out, and don't do it back to back, we'll never get caught.

I'm gettin' out the Benz with all eyes on me. Some stopped playin' ball, prostitutes are lookin' scared and lookin' my way like they want my money, hustlers have stopped their crap games just to view me. If I shout boo, they'd all jump. That's how much I'm in control over this joint. I nodded my head like yea' that's right with a cinnamon flavored tooth pick hangin' out the corner of my mouth. I got my black leather quarter inch trench coat on, my black turtleneck, my black jeans, and my black steel-toed boots. My grill's blingin' as I stretched my mouth as if to be glad to see my homey's. But inside I'm not, I could care less about all of em' even though I only cut for two of em'. I'm all about business not buddies.

I walked up on em' smokin' weed. "What up, ya'll ready to do this?"

One of em' spoke up quick. "Yea' let's bounce, I've been waitin' on this all day." He took another long drag off the joint and blew the smoke out of his mouth and nose at the same time. It rose up toward the side of the brick wall like a cloud. He dabbed the end of the joint against the wall and then put the rest of it in his pocket as if to save it. All the other fella's followed like they too scared to say somethin'.

We all packed in the car like it was a SUV. Better yet like we some sardines. Radio's bumpin' to my boy Diddy Diddy. Got it blastin' to sike us up for this quick journey. Got some sweet scent of some fresh weed foggin' up the inside of the car as it's thrustin' from our lips. Our revolvers hide between our stomachs and our belt buckles and the black masks are in our hands. Everything seems to be goin' right and nothin' could keep it from goin' wrong.

My cell just blew up. Everybody head turned in my direction like why now? I looked at em' and then at my cell like shut up, I'm in control. I looked at the screen to see that it's my lady. "Dawg' this Pricilla ya'll be easy." I turned the radio all the way down cause' Pricilla don't like my loud music goin' when I'm on the phone with her. "Yea' what up?"

"What chu' doin'?"

"Just chillin'. Why, what's up with chu'?"

"Nothin' that's why I'm callin' you. Where you at?"

"Ridin' with my boys."

"Come take me to the north side."

"Babe I can't do that right now. I'm bout' ta' handle some business."

"Who you care about the most, me or yo' so-call business?"

"Of course you babe, but..."

"But nothin', sound like you lovin' yo' boys more than you lovin' me?"

"There you go." I looked over at my boy Cross only to find him actin' like he's suckin' a pacifier. I threw up a finger that I dare not repeat.

"Look you got five minutes to get over here to take care of your women, or I'm gon' find somebody else to do it."

"Pricilla why you actin' like this, you know this ain't necessary? I'll be over their la...." The phone clicked into a dial tone.

I made a u-turn on my way to drop them back off like I just heard that my Moms just died.

"What's up man, why you buggin' out on us?" Cross said, high as a kite.

"Buggin', I ain't buggin' you get chu' a woman then tell me bout' buggin."

"I gotta' woman, but she ain't wearin' the pants like yo' woman is. Man she got chu' whipped."

"Look Cross you high and you startin' to talk too much. Every time you get high, you run yo' mouth on everybody's business, or you start talkin' bout' you see birds. Crazy. You know I'm quick to shoot chu' right?" He didn't say another word and nobody else did either.

I can feel bad bout' not fulfillin' our obligation, but I don't cause' I'll do anything for that woman. I'll look at it this way; she might've saved my life today.

؃

I just dropped the boy's off just like I picked em' all up. They got out the car fussin' cause' some of em' had bills to pay, and some of em' wanted to go get blowed tonight. So I guess I messed their rig up. I assured em' that tomorrow night's gon' be the night so be ready and ain't no coppin' out for me.

I looked down at my cell phone, pushed the button that got Pricilla's number already programmed in, and now I'm waiting to hear her voice.

"This Pricilla."

"Hey I'm on my way. You still mad at a brotha'?"

"Just a little bit."

"How can I make it up to you?"

"You'll see when you get here."

"I can't wait." She hung up in my face.

Maybe this' why I love this girl so much, she always like to play hard to get.

૦ઝ

I walked up to her high-rise penthouse condo over lookin' NY that I paid cold cash for, smiled, and stuck my chest out like I'm the man. All I pay is cash for my stuff. I figure my girl Pricilla's worth it.

There she go, standin' there with her long straight weave parted in the middle goin' straight down her back like some kinda' model straight from the hood and thangs. Straight gangsta' just like I like her. She got beautiful round thick lips, hot red lip stick with a lil' gloss on top, eye lashes flyin' out like feathers, hot red glitter pants outfit—the one that shows all that cleavage I like, a fresh tattoo she just got done with the words "JOE" stamp across her left titty, and some 6 inch pumps. Lookin' like a fire ball. I cracked a smile at the sight of what's mine and went up and hugged her real slow around her lower waist. She gave me a quick peck on the lips and brushed past me and went and got in the car. I don't even get mad no more cause' I know that's how she is. As long as I know she still love me that's all that matters. I got in. "Say what happen to makin' it up to me?"

"Stop bein' silly, you know I was just talkin' just to get you over here. I always make it up to you anyway. Look at all those new clothes you got in your closet."

"You right." I don't know why that woman intimidates me. Maybe it's because I love her so much and I'll do anything for her. She has a way of makin' me feel special in her own way. All the other chicks I mess with don't nearly make me feel the way she do. I know that's why I let her get away with so much. "Where am I takin' you?"

"To the 24 Hour Cleaners. I need to pick up my clothes."

I drove straight there mad cause' I could've been with my boys at the liquor store handlin' up on some business. Pricilla's the first female that I can be myself with. She just fired up some fresh smellin' weed, took a long drag, and handed it to me like she knows I'm gon' take a long drag off of it and hand it back to her. Which I did. She snickered underneath her breath and gave me a crazy look as the smoke came from her lips and fogged the air like a white cloud.

"Pricilla I'm goin' out tonight so get whatever you gotta' get now cause' when I'm busy, I'm busy."

"Just take me where I need to go now and I won't bother you no mo' tonight." She said. I let silence be my answer. She took another puff and blew it out as if to be a lil' ticked. She don't understand, she just want all my time and gets jealous when I don't give it to her. This thang' can be real strenuous if I let it, but I'm not cause' I got way too much work to do tonight.

I couldn't wait to take her where she needed to go. I dropped her off and now I'm callin' my boy Cross to let em' know its back on tonight. "Yo' Cross, it's back on tonight. Get the boys ready again, I ain't backin' out again this time."

"I'll let em' know but look playa' don't be backin' out on us again, we got bills to handle up on. You know we talked bad about chu'?"

"Man I could care less. Ya'll already know how Pricilla is so that shouldn't come as no shock."

"It ain't no shock, we just tired of the let downs that's all. We're tryin' to stick in there with chu' but to be honest we can't stand the brawd. She controls you too much."

"Yo' man you didn't have to come down hard on me like that?"

"I'm just tellin' you what the other fella's wanna' tell you. You need somebody to tell you the truth. Everybody's scared of you man. You know you run all these streets out here?"

"You know I do and I ain't gon' let nobody take em' over either. Do you hear me?"

"I hear ya' Joe man, but look, what's up for tonight?"

"That's what I wanted to call and tell you. It's on, we gon' go back to that same liquior store that we we're on our way to earlier."

"It's a done deal right? You ain't gon' bail out on us again are you?"

"Look man I told you that it's on. You startin' to make me mad."

"It's cool Joe man, we'll be waitin' when ever you show up." I hung up the phone in his face. I like em' when their scared, shows I got control over em'. Don't none of em' mess with me. That fool had the gumption to say that I was gon' bail out. Boy I tell ya' young bloods ain't got enough sense to know when they talkin' too much, but I do admire Cross for stickin' his chest out to tell me the truth.

 C3

As night fell fast, the city of ghetto fabulous partyin' has just begun. Everybody's hangin' out along the streets sellin' what ever they have from their possessions, to their hustlin', and shootin' the breeze back and forth with one another. I can't see myself with no other life but this. This' all I know and I'm used to bein' around. Like I said before Moms really showed me how to kiss death and step back from it. After I blow em' away, I step back and kiss the tip of my gun and step back from em'. I really don't have no sympathy for nobody either. I only do it when they're late in givin' me my money or messin' with one of my call girls. Sometimes I have a problem with jacked up hoodlems sleepin' with one of my girls and afterwards bail out on em' without payin' em'. That's when they wish they had of just done what they were supposed to do in the first place.

I rolled up to find the pose waitin' just like I told em' to. I squeezed my way between everybody standin' all over the street and pulled up along the curve with a fresh Black & Mild in my mouth, straight out of the carton. I see my man Cross got his gear on ready to do his thang. Cross brings a couple of new ones every time we roll out cause' he know they need the quick cash, and I don't question him cause' I know he knows who to bring and not to bring. The other young cats look like they just comin' to make em' a lil' change, to buy em' some new gear, or just to take care of their families. I ain't mad at em' though, I used to do the same thing when I rolled with the older cats back in the day. I let my window down as Cross walked up to the door. "Yo' what up?" I asked him. He didn't say anything. He and the three Cats just jumped in the car.

ော

I sped off skiddin' down the street like I had a destination to reach with everybody cheering like I'm a celebrity and thangs. That's how much respect I got. I see the police out doin' their thang' as we creeped through the deserted allies tryin' to find a place to lay my car. The liquoir store's lit up around the corner as usual. We creeped up in the dark ally with the light being the focal point inside of the store. I shut off the engine, grabbed one of the black skee masks Cross brought in his huge duffle bag, put it on; the fellas did the same thing as they followed my lead, made sure my guns in place—right between my stomach and my black jeans. I peaked at the face of my watch because it's the only source of light we got, checked the second hand for our que to go, reached for the latch with no fear in my heart. Cross and the others grabbed theirs and we quickly got out and ran up against this dark abandoned building. We each got our AK-47's cocked and loaded, ready to blow somebody's head off who would even step in our way.

Cross whispered to me, "Hey, just say the word and I'm goin' in."

"In five...four...three...two....one....go." We all took off runnin' in our own places. I went in first with my gat loaded, Cross stood at the door watchin' out while the clerk had his head turned listening to some music. The other Cats came in and went to the back of the store and set up on each end with both hands wrapped around a shot gun. When the clerk turned around, I ran up to the counter with my mask on and pointed my gun right between his eyes, daring him to move. Cross came around me and went straight for the cash register while one of the Cats went and took his place. I'm screamin',

Cross' screamin', and the clerk's screamin', beggin' us not to take his life. I could care less cause' I've done it before so it really don't matter if I do it again. Cross got the money and threw it in the duffle bag and quickly nodded his head like let's go. One of the Cats yelled the code for the police, we ran out, ran back to the get away car, and took off like the police was already after us. I sped down the street with my foot smashin' the peddle to the floor, zippin' in and out of traffic. Everybody's takin' their stuff off while the music's blastin'. We laughin' cause' the plan went straight. "Everybody was in their right places! Ya'll made me proud!" They all burst out laughin'. I know they're glad I said what I said cause' that's how much they admire me and how much they're scared of me. Cross fired up some fresh weed.

"I can't wait to see how much we got! Look like we got way more than what we got the last time eventhough it was just a lil' ol' store."

I glanced over at the huge duffle bag we used to put the money in as Cross ran his fingers through it. I smiled to agree with him, and turned into the projects. We went straight to our favorite place to count the money—an abandoned, empty stank hole of a building, divided the money among us which wasn't nothin' but $100's between us, and left goin' in our own directions. I know it ain't big bank cash but it's good, quick in and out doe.

ᔕ

I drove down the street with a smile on my face thinkin' bout' what I can get for my lady. Got a lil' change in my pocket—at least enough to get her a diamond tennis bracelet and a nice silky red negligee—my favorite color. I'll handle that tomorrow. I went to my lil' project pad. Most would be surprised that I don't have a huge mansion in some big time neighborhood, but I don't like people to guess what I got so I like to keep it on the down low. Pricilla's been beggin' to move in with me. I think I'm gon' let her cause' I can't stand bein' away from her not a minute. Her phone rang one time—I can tell she's waiting. "Hello Miss. Beautiful."

She snickered, "How are you?"

"I'm cool. Business is done."

"I see. So what's up now?"

"I want you to move out of your pad."

She started screamin', "When?"

"Now." She hung up the phone in my face and called right back like she didn't mean to do it. "Yea' what's up, why you hang up in my face?"

"I didn't mean to, I got too excited!" She screamed the woman's scream.

"Don't worry bout' gettin' all your stuff tonight, just get enough and we'll move the rest tomorrow. I'll have the movers come and handle all that just do what I say." For the first time she's submissive. She's finally lettin' me be a man. I know it ain't gon' last long though, it's goin' too good.

"Are you on your way?"

"Yea' just be ready when I get there." She agreed as we both hung up the phone. I'm excited and I know she is too.

❧

As soon as I pulled up in her condo driveway, I didn't even have to call, she came out with a huge travel bag in her arms, her purse caught between em', and a huge smile on her face.

She jumped in the car and gave me a big, slow kiss on my lips. "Hey baby, I'm so glad you finally made that move. Now I feel like we can have somethin' together."

I looked at her, "Is that what you felt?"

"Yea', I felt like you just wanted a part time woman. You wanted me when you wanted me." She said, tryin' to have a lil' ol' attitude.

"Now Pricilla, babie what gave you that idea?" I slowly put my hand on her thigh to comfort her but she moved it. I see she's back to her high-strong attitude. And that's what's makin' me hate that I ever asked her.

She gave me this stern look. "Because you never wanted me to come to your house. I felt like you were using me."

"I'll never use you babie. I love you, don't chu' know that?" I slightly grabbed her chin and kissed her again.

She cracked a smiled as if she wanted to believe it. That is my words and the kiss, she knows that's real. "So with those words you not gon' kick a sista' out once I get over there?"

"I wouldn't have asked you to move in with me."

"Alright then." She stuffed her purse inside of her travel bag.

ʊ

The car was silent all the way over there. She didn't say a word and I didn't either. Our thoughts were our conversation with the only thing doin' the talkin' is her hand caressing my hand locked in hers. It's like we allowin' our hands to create a symphony. I pulled up and parked as usual. She got her bag; I got my stuff, and walked up to the apartment. We went in and got comfortable and situated.

ʊ

As I put my stuff down, the thought of the life I'm living just flashed before my eyes. It was so real it made me sit down on the side of the bed and think. Pricilla could careless she's just glad to be up in my house. She's just too controlling. I need a woman that's sensitive and loving. One who cares about my feelings and my needs. I don't know how long I can do this. But I love this chick. We got a lot of history. Been through a lot of stuff and came through it and still together. The more the night goes on, I'm hatin' that I asked her to move in. It's cool. I'll see how this' gon' turn out. I can always put her out.

Ch. 2

I couldn't wait to get back home from Cross's to make her feel like a real woman, especially after she told me how she felt about me treatin' her like a part time woman. The thought of what I wanted to do last night spoke back to my mind again. I ran by this sweet smellin' Joint the ladies love. Got soap, shampoo, lotion, and bikini's—all that stuff that makes us Cats go crazy.

As soon as I walked through the door, this Indian brawd almost tackled me excited about givin' me her business. "Can I help you?" She stuck her hand out to welcome me.

"Yea'." I looked at her hand crazy; like calm down. "Yea' I'm lookin' for somethin' sweet and special for my lady."

"What kind of special?"

She walked over to toward the rack of garments. "How about some negligee'?" She lifted up a red negligee' and pushed it towards me like it was already mine.

"Yea', now that's the word I'm talkin' bout'." I took it out of her hand. "But don't leave out the smell goods." We walked over to the lotion section.

"Ok, how about some of this Strawberry Kiwi lotion?" She took it off the shelf and handed it to me for a quick sniff.

"That's cool." I gave it back to her. "But I need somethin' that's gon' last all night long. This ain't no pop and go show."

She laughed and fanned herself. "O' my, you're somethin' else. Ok what about this sweet smelling, all night lasting perfume and lotion, you can spray and rub it on her?" She throwed at me a sneaky smile.

I looked at her like, alright now chill out. I'm hip to yo' game. I know you tryin' to make a sell. She got the nerve to have this pretty Indian, golden color, 5'7 frame, nice round hips, and some high Indian cheek bones; and beautiful long coal straight black hair. Almost make a brotha' wanna' holler at her if I wasn't in the mood for my ol' lady Pricilla. I took it out of her hand, took one sniff, and knew it was the right one. "I'll take it."

"Great! I knew you wouldn't disagree. She's going to love them. This silky negligee is one of our limited editions, and it's the last one we have left in stock. She must really be special?"

"Trust me, she's all that."

We walked up to the cash register, she did her thang with the cash register and put my goods in the shoppin' bag, and I did mine with poppin' out the cash she needed to make the transaction complete. She got what she wanted—cash, and I got what I wanted—the red negligee and some sweet smellin' perfume and lotion.

C3

I drove the streets like a felon bein' chased by the police. I'm in that much of a hurry to get home and get it on her and to sniff her all night long.

C3

I walked in to the place smellin' like a home cooked meal. Man, ain't nothin' like a black woman in the kitchen cookin' a home cooked meal of some good ol' soul food for a brotha'.

I walked in the kitchen strugglin' to her dazzy's cuttin' across her butt—teasin' me, and a sleeveless tank top with no bra on makin' her breast more noticeable. I pulled the bags behind me and reached my lips for her lips. She met em' with a smile and a nosy what chu' got behind yo' back eye. "Hey baby." I pulled her close to me with one arm and the other still behind my back with the bags.

"Hey, what's behind your back?"

"I'll tell you when you tell me what's that smell comin' from the stove?"

"I'm makin' my baby some roast, with some cabbage, some candy yams, and some buttered corn bread." She smiled real hard like, yea' I'm the woman. "Now tell me what's behind your back?" She tried to reach but I stopped her.

"I'll show you in a minute." She smacked her lips, gave me a slow peck, and went back to cookin'.

"I'm goin' to the room. I need some time alone so don't come in for bout' a minute."

"Your wish is my command Chief." She winked her eye, pullin' the corn bread from the stove.

"I like's that. Chief huh'? Alright, hope you keep sayin' that in a minute." I took my trench off, threw it on the couch, spit the cinnamon tooth pick out, and went to prepare the room.

Got the hot bubble bath thang' goin' and spreaded some rose peddles all around the room—even some across the bed, even though they gon' get thrown off anyway. I laughed to myself. I sprayed just a little of my favorite cologne Pricilla loves on the sheets and pillow to tease the mood a little, and laid her silky negligee with my favorite red bottom pumps beside em' on the arm of the jacuzzi tub serenaded with candles. I turned the bathroom lights off.

As soon as I walked back in the kitchen I was met with a hot, long kiss. She couldn't wait, must've sensed what I was doin'; which got her in the mood. She tore my button-down shirt open and continuously kissed me down my hairy chest as we made our way to the bedroom. I took her clothes off and helped her into the tub. I had to get in with her after taking one look at her beautiful body. I sat behind her and filled the towel with water as I carefully washed her back and other spots, and let it drip from the top of her neck down to the lower parts of her back. She sighed like she had a long day and needed this. The steam from the hot bath water made us sweat together.

ೞ

I'm layin' on the bed with no shirt on in my red silky boxers waitin' to see what my prize looks like. She opened the door to the bathroom, slowly cat walked out like a model on the runway, and ran right into my arms. I couldn't wait to receive her. I knew the negligee would fit just right. "You look great." I slowly said choosing each word before I give em' to her.

"Thanks to my Chief." She whispered.

"No, thank you for makin' me feel like a real man. You cook, keep this house clean, and then you know how to make me feel like a real man." I almost teared up with her in my arms, but the tears didn't fall cause' I'm too hard.

"I just wanna' please you. You're so good to me. You take care of me, you love me the right way, you try to act all hard but chu' so romantic. Joe look at all these rose peddles. And the bed smells so good to me right now—my favorite cologne." She leaned over and slightly sniffed the pillow. I couldn't help but reach with her. I slowly ran my hand down her back, took her negligee off; leaving only the red bottom pumps on, and started massaging her body from head to toe with some baby oil. The lights went out to a love zone; and the rest is history as usual. This chick is so fine I'll never give up on this. After all I just done, I know she ain't got no beef with stayin' with me now. And I ain't got no beef with her stayin' here either, as long as she keep doin' what she doin'—pleasin' a brotha'.

○ℰ

I heard Pricilla talkin' to one of her girls on the phone. Must be talkin' bout' me cause' she whisperin'. "You ain't gotta' whisper." I walked over and laid across her lap as she casually sat on my long sofa.

"Joe why won't chu' move, you see I'm on the phone?" She went back to talkin' to who ever. I just laid there and listened, just like a big ol' baby.

○ℰ

I laid there until she finished which was about an hour later. I know she know I heard everything. Probably wanted me to hear. Especially the part when she said, "we gon' come and visit the church I just need to talk to him about it first."

"Talk to who about what?" I asked. I barley opened one eye and cracked a smile lettin' her know she can't get nothin' over on me.

She looked at me crazy cause' she thought I was still sleep. "You are so nosey. You need to get chu' a life."

"I'm tryin' too but somebody won't let me. Every time I'm runnin' with my boys you chasen' me down tryin' to keep a man home bound."

She looked at me crazy again. "That's because I know what ya'll do. I'm not tryin' to trap you Joe if that's what you think.

24

I just don't want nothin' to happen to you. Your life is so dangerous. Somebody can kill you at any moment and who am I gon' be left with? Nobody. That's why I want you to come out of that thuggish life style. You need to go to church." She got up and started walking towards the kitchen.

I followed her with my three cents. "How you gon' tell me bout' goin' to church and you don't go?"

"I'm about to start," she turned to face me. "Look Joe I know I haven't been the best person that I can be. I made some mistakes in my life, one is bein' a call girl for you—sellin' my body to who ever. Smokin' up some weed, and drinkin' my life away. I'm tired and I'm fixin' to try and make a change whether you with me or not." I fired up a blunt right in her face to see if she was for real. "You ain't gotta' do that Joe cause' it ain't gon' work. I've made my mind up. I'm about to make a change for the better." She went and dropped down on the couch like it was gon' catch her. I just watched her from the bar. I ain't gon' run behind her.

"Who got cho' mind all confused?" I ran back in the bedroom and snatched her cell phone and started lookin' at the numbers one by one. "Ain't no nigga' gon' take my woman. I'll kill em' before I let that happen." She ran in the room and tried to grab the phone out of my hand but I grabbed her hand before she could and threw her down on the bed.

"Joe you ain't gotta' do me like that!" She yelled. "Give me my phone!" She yelled and tried to reach for it again.

"What's wrong now, huh'? This' the kind of stuff you do to me! Now you see how it feels huh'?" I kept on lookin' at the numbers but they all look familiar except one, so I called it. A female picked up on one ring. "Who dis'?"

"Hello?" She said. Her voice is calm.

"I said who dis'?"

"This' Sabrina."

"Who's Sabrina?" Pricilla looked at me crazy and ran out of the room to me lookin' like the biggest fool in the world.

"I'm Sabrina's friend from church."

"Sabrina don't go to church so what nigga' you callin' for?"

"I'm sorry when you wanna' talk to me in a respectful manner, you're welcome to call me back." She hung up in my face.

I looked at the phone. Ain't no woman ever hung up the phone in my face. I called her right back. "Why you hang up in my face?"

"Are you ready to talk sensible?" Pricilla came back in the room smiling. I put on my macho look not lettin' her know that I'm embarrassed.

"Just tell me who you are?" I toned my voice down.

"I guess I'll answer you since you've finally calmed down. I'm Pricilla's friend. I live right around the corner from her.

She's about to start coming with me to church. Why don't you come with her?"

"Church ain't for me."

"What do you mean?"

"I'm sayin' that me and church don't get a long. They wouldn't accept somebody like me no way."

"Why do you say that?"

"Cause' I've seen em'. They laugh at people like me."

"What kind of person are you?"

"I'm a straight up thug from the streets."

"And?"

"And. And so they wouldn't accept me."

"Have you tried?"

"Yea' I tried and I'll never try again. Me and some of my boys went, and they talked bad about us. Said we wasn't dressed right, and we smelt bad cause' we just smoked some weed before we went in. They tried to make us sit way in the back of the church, but we left. *(2 Timothy 3:5)* Foolish stuff like that make me hate the church. Cross nem' got me oughta' there before I shot somebody cause' I'm the kind of Cat that will shoot with no remorse. So from that day forward I said I would never go to a church again for somebody to say somethin' crazy to me. Everybody in the church ain't got it all together like you think they do. I know they packin' guns just like me. Probably had one on em' the day I went." She stayed quiet. "O' now you ain't gon' say nothin'?" I laughed. "That's

a trip when you start talkin' bout' church folks they get quiet."
Pricilla went to the bathroom and started fixin her hair like she
ain't listenin' which I know she is.

"I'm not a church folk." She said. Still calm.

"Hah' I got chu', now I'm waitin' on the church attitude!"

"I don't have an attitude. As a matter of fact, I understand
your pain."

"Pain? I ain't got no pain."

"Ok well I understand your disappointment with the
church."

"How can you understand my disappointment you don't
even know me?"

"I don't have to know you. I can hear it."

"O' so you some kind of expert now huh'?"

"No I'm just listening to you talk and by the way you talk,
and from your tone, I can tell that they really hurt you."

"You might be right." Pricilla had the nerve to laugh from
around the corner while she picked at her hair. I started to go
and jack her butt up but I changed my mind. "Ain't nobody
ever talked to me this calm before not even my woman. Why
you so calm especially after the way I've been talkin' to you?"

"Words don't hurt me. They used to but that was before I
got delivered from people." She stopped to see what I was
about to say, but I only cleared my throat to hide being
intimidated. I can't let no woman know I'm intimidated by

her. "I've been hurt right in the church just like you have, actually worse."

"How can yours be worse than mine?"

"I was put to an open shame by the pastor. He heard that I was sleeping with one of the deacons in the church and called me out during service. I couldn't believe it. I was so embarrassed. I ran out crying and never went back."

Man I'm started to feel sorry for this brawd. "Were you guilty?"

"No I wasn't, at least not with that one." I laughed. I can tell she smiled a little. "I never had any dealings with him none what-so-ever and that's what hurt because, number one, they were false accusations; and two, because of the way the pastor went by it. He called me out all in front of the congregation (2 Timothy 3:10-17). I know it had something to do with the fact that he knew my past and it took one lying spirit to come and lie on me and he believed them instead of seeking the Lord and seeing what was the real truth. That's why every church needs a Spirit fed pastor. A pastor that's after God's own heart. One who knows the voice of God, obeys Him, loves God's people, and is not stuck on himself and what he wants; and does not follow after false voices and doctrines and what they think (John 10:27).

"Did some laugh?"

"Some laughed and some didn't. Most made the woo sound. It was horrible. I felt like a prostitute in the church and for a minute there it made me feel like I had almost done something wrong. I almost ran up there and knocked him out, but I chose to just run out (John 8:7)."

"I guess there's hater's everywhere."

"Yea' there is. You can't lift up nobody—not even a pastor. You can respect his position, but don't ever lift him or her up higher than God because God is the only One you should lift up *(John 12:32)*. God is a jealous God *(Exodus 20:5, Nahum 1:2)*. And He gets all the glory *(1 Corinthians 10:31)*. That's why you have to live your own life and work out your own soul salvation *(Philippians 2:12-13)*. You can't go by what has happened to you in the past, you gotta' leave your past behind and keep on going *(Isaiah 43:18)*. It took a while for me to heal, in fact, for a while I gave up the church building and the people. I just watched it on TV and on the internet until I felt convicted and started goin' back to church, but goin' from church to church, because I was still scared to join one. But I finally got tired and prayed and asked God what church would He have for me to attend and He led me right to the church that I'm at right now. If I would've given up, I don't know where I would be today. Now I love my church, they don't judge, and the Pastor is nothing like the other one. God has truly assured my prayers. I watch how my Pastor loves the church, the clergy and staff. He encourages them and lets them exercise their spiritual gifts. I know you don't understand what I'm saying but maybe one day you will. But as I was saying, sometimes when there's a great anointing on somebody's life and God begans to raise that minister up, and the congregation begins to want to hear from that minister, the pastor tries to get jealous and not let that minister go forth. Crazy. I'll never understand that. If I didn't love the Lord, I'd a given up on these pastors that's hooked on themselves, ingulfed in their pride, hiding in their own sins, and don't follow God and the church a long time ago."

"You needed to say that, didn't you?" I cut her off.

"Yea' I did."

"You didn't have a problem with how you looked in the church?"

"When I first started goin' to church I did. I didn't have a lot of clothes and I used to where the same ones over and over every Sunday. They had big holes and some food marks on em' where I couldn't get out even after I washed them, so I just wore em' anyway. There were even times when I didn't have any money to wash my clothes and had to wear em' dirty. They laughed and snickered every time I hit the door. They wouldn't let me sit in the front. They didn't wanna' use me in the ministry. I didn't have any friends or caring so-called sisters because they all had their own lil' clicks, hidden agenda's, and they were too embarrassed to be around me. There were a few that spoke to me and went on about their business. So see there, you ain't the only one that's been hurt in the church."

"Naw' I guess not. But you don't understand my life style. I've killed people before, I rob liquor stores, sell drugs, prostitute women, and control and own women."

"And so, what's there to understand?"

"I'm a thug and a hustla' lady. People don't receive thugs like me. They judge me and they scared of me."

"God loves thugs too." She said with a loving tone *(1 John 4:11-12)*.

"You think so?"

"Yep I sure do."

"You think He would accept a Thug like me, all that I do and don' done wrong?"

"Everybody's done wrong. Infact we've all sinned and come short of God's glory, but He doesn't deny us. He draws us to Him *(Romans 3:23)*.

"So what I gotta' do first?"

"Surrender your life to Him."

"How do I do that?"

"Repent and then give up the life style that you're living and live for Him."

"O' man, that's a hard one. I can't just quit just like that. I got too much ridin'—my boys, my money, my bills, my call girls, I got an underground establishment if you know what I mean?"

"I hear what you're saying, but you asked and I told you. You can't live two lives when you live for the Lord. It has to be all of Him or nothing at all."

"Well I ain't gon' even play with Em' cause' I ain't ready. I got way too much ridin' on me."

"Well it's your choice. I believe you'll come when you get enough."

"Whata' you mean by that?"

"When I got tired of being sick and tired, I gave Him my life. That means, when I got tired of lettin' men lay all on me, got tired of smokin' weed and sniffin' coke, and lettin' it make my mind do crazy thangs. I got tired of lookin' any kind of way, and my life down to rock bottom, I ran to Jesus with my hands up with the quickness. And I believe this' what you'll do. When you really need Him, you'll come runnin'."

"Alright then, you keep believin' that."

She snickered underneath her breath and replied as if I never said anything. "Ok nice talking to you and hope to hear back from you. I talk to Pricilla all the time and now I think I have another friend."

"You probably won't hear back from me. I don't have female friends other than my woman." When I looked up at Pricilla she had this huge grin on her face. I know that made her feel special cause' she always accusin' me of lovin' on other women other than her.

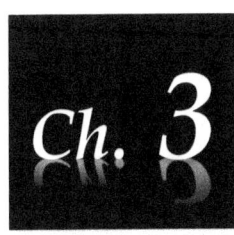

While Pricilla's takin' her a shower I got some time to think about why my life just flashed before me. That ain't never happened to me before. I've always felt comfortable doin' all the wrong thangs with no conviction. It's almost like somebody's been on their knees for me—must be that chick. I know it can't be my Moms cause' she's always all cracked out. And I know it ain't Pricilla cause' she wouldn't have ever moved up in here—so I think. I got one hand under my chin tryin' to think this thang through but my thoughts just don't seem to be comin' together. All I could see was me shootin' and killin' somebody, and then somebody turnin' and shootin' me dead. Then all I remember was fallin' down this huge dark hole with fire at the bottom waitin' on me to land. It was crazy. Almost makes me wanna' go to somebody church. That's how scared I am. What I'm gon' do? I can't tell her. She'll never understand. But maybe she would. She came out of the shower with no clothes on as I laid across the bed. I barely looked at her. This' crazy. I ain't never felt bad about livin' with no woman I wasn't married to *(I Corinthians 10:8)*. This' somethin' that everybody does. Shack up. It ain't nothin' that we think about especially not the fact that it's wrong. Pricilla came and sat beside me and started rubbin' my lower back. I guess cause' she see that I'm deep in thought. "What's wrong?"

I stood up. "I don't know. How you feel about movin' up in here?"

"I love it. What's wrong, havin' a change of heart?" I didn't say nothin'. She just looked at me like she was waitin' for this. "I see you didn't mean what you asked me?" She started puttin' on some clothes and gettin' her things together.

"Pricilla stop. I want you to stay. I just wanted to know what you thought."

"You already know my thoughts." She slowly took back off what little clothes she put on, and threw her things on the floor.

"You right. I do know your thoughts. Look it's cool. Hey make me some eggs and bacon."

"It's too late for all that. I'm goin' to bed." She went and got in the bed like what I just asked didn't even matter. This' why I can't do this anymore. Man what I'm gon' do? I don't think I can get rid of her now. I like to come and go. I think she gon' wanna' know my every move like somebody. I ask myself, why do I stay with this woman? Maybe it's because she's such a challenge. I ain't never had no challenge like this before.

"I'm leavin', I'll be back." I tried giving her a kiss but she turned her head.

"Where you goin'?"

"I'm going to talk to Cross for a lil' while."

"How long you gon' be?"

"Not long." I walked out the room going towards the front door.

She came and slightly pulled on my trench coat tryin' to make me stay. "I want you to stay with me." She softly said.

"Look Pricilla I told you that I'm gon' go talk to Cross for a while. The way you actin' makes wonder why I ever asked you to move in. See this' what I'm talkin' bout'. This' why I ain't quick to ask no woman to marry me." She left me alone and went back to the room. I walked out hatin' that I said what I said and did what I did.

℞

I left goin' down the early morning dark streets with no destination to reach. I had to lie to her. I had to get out of that joint. I rubbed the back of my bald head to gather my thoughts. Not the thought of why I asked her to move in with me, but the thought of what flashed before my eyes. Maybe I need to get my life together. I ain't never felt bad like this. And I can't shake it either. The thoughts of me robbin' and shootin' all those people keep runnin' through my mind. Their screams and pleas of wantin' me to stop that gave me a rush. I didn't care back then, but somehow I'm startin' to show a little concern. Maybe this was a warning from the Man UpStairs? He does speak to sinners, callin' them out of their sin (*Matthew 9:13*). I heard this on TV once but didn't pay it no mind up until now. He must have somethin' for me to do. But how could He ever save a thug like me? How could He ever use a thug like me? I didn't think God like thugs? Nobody likes thugs. The world don't even like the way we look, nor the way we talk, nor the things that we do. So if they don't like us, how will this God (*Acts 10:34*) (*1 John 4:7-21*)? My heart is hurting. I can't tell nobody. It gets hard tryin' to keep this bad boy image for everybody. My heart is burnin' on the inside, hidden from the world cause' the world don't care bout' no thug. They think we all bad people. I can't be nobody but myself. I didn't grow up in Beverly Hills with a silver spoon in my mouth. I had to survive on these coal hearted streets called life. The life of crime, drugs, and lives bein' taken right before my eyes—constantly. My crack head momma never told me about this Man called Jesus. I had to hear about Em' from another source—the TV. And I think all they talk about is a lie. Saw somebody one time hittin' somebody in the head and they fell out and got up shoutin', talkin' bout' God is good and how God loves them. I was mad the rest of the night cause' I couldn't believe that they would hit that woman in the head and say that Jesus is love. Man that's crazy. If God is so real then why He wouldn't let my Pops do right and be in my life? Why He let my Moms get hooked on crack and smoke her life away? And why I ain't got no contact with all my other sista's and brotha's? These are questions that need answers. My drive turned into a three hour ride. I never went over Cross's. I never had intentions to. I just told her that so I could get out of the house. I think I need to get me a real job and stop all this gang bangin' and the rest of the life style that I'm livin'. I drove back determined with the early mornin' sun smilin' at me.

ᘉ

Pricilla's asleep—so I think. I walked in the room to a slight sun ray kissing across the bed. She got her back turned away from me. She could have her eyes open. If I know her, she's up listenin' and waitin' on an explanation. But she ain't gettin' one. I slowly laid down beside her hopin' I wouldn't wake her up but don't think its workin'. I slowly rolled over on her side, slid my hand around her lower waist until my hand locked on the other side. She braced herself as if to be mad but didn't say nothin'.

ᘉ

I haven't told nobody that I'm thinkin' about tryin' to change my life and get me a good job and stop robbin' the liquior stores, smokin' weed, and drinkin' like I don't care whether I live or die. Kizzy's Janitorial Service just came in my visual view. Look like they're hiring. I ain't never had no job before.

Never had a reason to. Always had money in my pocket. Got my women doin' my business for me, robbin' for a piece of change, and the rush of it. Controling everybody around me.

It's the heat of the day and this up coast weather ain't allowin' me to give up my trench coat. I wear it with almost everything. I walked in and asked the heavey-set, blond hair white clerk for an application. She hesitated with an attitude but gave it to me as if to be scared that I would rob her if she didn't. I wanna' tell her to stop smackin' that gum before her lips fall off. Ain't nobody gon' do nothin' to her. I sat on one of the six empty seats they have lined up against the wall with an attitude she just gave me, filled out the application to the best of my ability, and gave it back to her. She quickly took it, looked it over, and said that they would call me as soon as the application has been processed. Before I could walk out, the boss man came up to her booth and took the application from her and called me by my name. I turned and walked back over to em'. He kept lookin' at the application as if to be contemplating as to whether or not he wants to give me the job or not. He's an average built black man with a long coal black, bushy beard, short curly fro with speckles of gray linin' around the front, and a stern look to go with it. Looks to be in his late forties or early fifties. His loud green pants and yellow shirt almost makes a person believe that it's a uniform but it seems to be his style of dress. I had to cut a smile.

"I see here that you've never worked before?" He asked as the clerk looked at me crazy. I know she don't want me to get the job.

"Um' naw' I ain't never worked befo'."

He kept looking at the application. "Come see me in the morning at eight and be ready to work."

I looked at him, cracked a hard smile—one I ain't gave in a long time, stuck my tongue out at the attendant; lettin' her know she didn't get her wish. I walked out. I can't believe a thug is about to get a real nine to five for a janitorial service. Wait til' Cross hear this. I dialed his number as soon as I got in the car. "Yo' man what's the deal?"

"O' I can't call it. You sound like you just robbed another store?"

"Naw' man I just got a nine to five." I took off down the street.

"What? Man you gotta' be crazy. When did you do this?"

"Just now." I said, slowing down to traffic.

"Look man, Joe you can't keep this job, its gon' mess us up by you bein' in the system and thangs. And what happened to you sayin' that you would never get a nine to five?"

"Well people change." The phone got quiet. I know he's in disbelief. Cross ain't never heard me talk like a whimp. "It's just somethin' I feel like I need to do."

"No it ain't! You messin' up the rig we got goin'! Do you even care that this' how I make my livin'?"

"Look, I care but I ain't tryin' to go this way for the rest of my life. You got the rest of the other fella's, you can do it without me."

"But it ain't gon' be the same Joe and you know it. Everybody follows yo' lead dawg."

My mind is wonderin' at the thought of the position that I'll be loosin' and all the attention that I get from the women. "I'm gon' see what Pricilla say."

"Pricilla?"

"Yea' man that's my lady. I care bout' what she thinks."

"Man you weak."

"Who you callin' weak? Don't play with me Cross you know I'll come over there and kill you dead." He got quiet cause' he knows I'm for real. "Now I thought I'd call you cause' you supposed to be my boy and I thought you'd be happy for me."

"Joe man I can't even front. I can't be happy for you cause' once a thug always a thug. And we don't get nine to fives, we hustle for what we want—and you know that." I just listened. "So what's gon' be of us?" My mouth won't move cause' I don't know what to tell em'. "I guess you don' gave up on us?"

"I ain't gave up on ya'll. This' somethin' that I gotta' do."

"I bet that Pricilla's responsible for this. She always finds a way to pull you away from us."

"This ain't got nothin' to do with Pricilla. I'm my own man. Don't no woman control me."

"Well I can't tell."

"Cross you gettin' too mouthy."

"Look Joe how you think I'm supposed to react, huh'? You call me and drop this news on me like a ton of bricks and expect me to be with you? I can't do it. The thug life needs you. You see it for yo' self. Look at how everybody looks at chu'? When you step into the hood, everybody's head turn— waitin' to hear what chu' gotta' say. Waitin' to receive from you Joe, you. Man so…"

"And that's why I gotta' job because I'm tired of the thangs that they receivin' from me. I'm tired of sendin' people to hell by my words and the drugs I've already given them. I know the Man Upstairs don't like us right now." I can't believe thoughs words came out of my mouth. I want to believe what I just said but I don't know how.

"Man what? What don' happened to you? You been lettin' some fake Christian brain wash you *(Romans 14:11)?* I ain't never heard you talk like this. The Man UpStairs, where did that come from?"

"From my heart, Cross." I said, tryin' to convince myself that what I'm doin' and sayin' is right.

"Man you sound real soft. Don't no thug talk like that!" He yelled through the phone. I can't tell Cross that I don't wanna' be no thug no mo'. He wouldn't understand. I can't explain to

43

my own self the change that's goin' on on the inside of me. I just feel different and I don't know why. Maybe like I said before, somebody must be prayin' for me. I wonder who it is—probably that chick.

ca

I was bright and early to work like a Hebrew slave. The man told me to be there at 8:30am, but I was there at 8. Wanna' see what this' gon' be like. Maybe Cross was right when he said the Thug life needs me. I'm havin' second thoughts. With my first thought bein' the ring leader. So I'm a go with the ring leader.

I walked into the small glass windowed office building, the secretary made her presence known by her white silhouette. She must be preparing everything to open the business up. My pace slowed down cause' I'm not ready to face her attitude. Got a bad one too. Better be glad I'm determined to see what this' all about cause' I would blow her head off at the drop of a dime. I pulled the handle of the door, she jumped like I gotta' gun.

"O' so you're on time?" She said sarcastically without a smile.

"I'm befo' time." I walked up to the counter and put both hands on the counter.

"Doesn't mean anything, you're not going to move up the latter."

"Look you blond brawd, I just wanna' work, stay out of my way. Ain't got no beef with you."

She brushed me off with her hands and had the nerve to roll her eyes. She a bold brawd. Must want me to turn her flips and end her life. I sat down on one of the six chairs sittin' up against the wall and waited for the boss man. He finally walked in with a brief case in one hand, and what look like a lunch kit in the other one. His suit lit up the room with a loud blue from head to toe, to be noticed. I gotta' give it to em' it's tight, it fits an ol' man like him. He still ain't no Gee, just a wanna' be. My trench is my suit. I don't need that to make me look like a business man with a lotta' paper. I let the paper make me look good.

"Hey!" I stood up. He stuck his hand out for a hand shake, all professional and thangs. "You ready to work?"

"Yeah' Boss Man?" I met his hand shake with mine.

"Boss Man? I like that. Ain't nobody ever called me Boss Man." He looked at Ms. Blondie as she frowned ugly. I tripped out.

"I call it like it is."

"Ok cool. I likes that. Look like you gon' be alright here." He reached for my hand shake and I gave it to him firm like a man again. Gotta' watch em' cause' he'll be ready to fire off on a Gee and fire me in a minute if I slip up. "Follow me to my office."

I walked behind him like a poodle ready to see what he has for me. "What's my first move?"

"What?"

"First move."

"I don't know that kind of language."

I had to crack a smile. Thought he was from the hood by the way he talk. Guess I was wrong. "I'm sayin' what do you have for me to do first?"

"O' ok. Well let's see here. There's plenty for you to do. Just tryin' to see what you can do first." He started rumblin' through his papers on his messy desk. "O' ok, here's your first assignment." He reached over and grabbed some orange overalls, some keys from off the chair next to his desk, and then handed me three sheets of paper with what look like a map on one of em'. "Go there." He pointed at the map. "And be back here by 12 noon for your next assignment. Don't go nowhere else—not even to the bathroom. Need you to clean every crack in every corner, the instructions are on one of those three sheets of paper I just gave you. And remember the car is not for joy ridin', it's for business only."

I didn't say nothin', just walked out lookin' like a female maid hatin' that I'm tryin' to turn my life around. Man, the haunt of me as a thug turnin' from the bad life to what seem like the good life is comin' back to pull me back. When I wanna' do right, evil is always present. *(Romans 7:21, Entire Chapter 7)*

CB

As soon as I got to the warehouse, took one look at the filth I was told to clean, I turned around and ran out and skidded back to the office and sat out in the parkin' lot thinkin', this' crazy. "Naw' man, I gotta' do this. I'm doin' this for my lady." I said to myself. I turned the small blue Escort back around wanting to fire up a blunt but I'm hesitant cause' the smell would leave a scent. I headed back to the warehouse— determined until my determined got weak when I pulled in the parking lot. Cars are everywhere. Only a few folks are goin' and comin'. Not a very popular office building.

I skidded into a parking space like I was late. Got out, popped the trunk to get the cleaning stuff, and just as I closed the trunk of this raggedy Escort, everything went in slow motion on me as this fine, long, coal black rolla' set, mini skirt, black pump wearin' brawd just walked past the car goin' towards the front door of the building; twisting like she know I'm lookin'. The cleanin' stuff slipped out of my hand like they had grease on em'. She kept walking and went inside of the building like she didn't hear my cleanin' stuff drop to the ground. I rushed and picked em' up from off the ground and tried to catch up with her but when I got inside, hit the elevator, she was nowhere to be found.

The smell of the old building added to the scent of the dirty mop water sittin' over in the corner of the lobby like it's waitin' for me. I stretched my lips. Sweat poured from my temple as the 110 degree temperature that I'm exaggerating too. There's no dought that the air is broke. This office building's way too clean to be this hot. Crazy. They need to report this. This' a mess, look like the janitor services went on strike from cleanin' this buildin'. Where do a brotha' start? Boss Man told me not to miss a corner, so here we go. I walked down the hall into the bathroom of one of the office rooms and found pee all around the toilet bowl. I held my nose and threw the towel in the toilet as hard as I could and got out of there, but had to turn right back around and do my job.

It seems impossible to clean every corner. A Gee ain't never had to clean like no maid befo', but I'm determined to change my life. I just need some help. I say this on the inside cause' I don't wanna' look like I'm soft. I know my man Cross would laugh. All he know is that I got a job. Man if I told him that I'm into the maid service, that fool would laugh for days and my respect would too.

I'm rollin' the cleaning equipment and the mop bucket down this skinny hall that's fit for one person; sweatin' like a construction worker. I wiped my forehead, took a long sigh, and met a long icy cold glass of water as I turned to clean my last office. I dig how her long pink finger nails are wrapped around the icy glass as the sweat of water's runnin' between her fingers.

"Here you go, thought you might could use this." She handed it to me and smiled.

As soon as I caught eyes with her, I couldn't help but remember that beautiful familiar lookin' face. "Hey don't I know you?" She walked away as if to be in a hurry to get somewhere. Two fine brawd's in the same office building. A brotha' can't find that nowhere else. That's very rare.

She glanced back but kept walking. "No I don't think so."

I caught up with her as hot as it is and with this trench coat makin' it worse. "I believe I do know you. I can prove it if you let me talk to you."

"Don't have time, got a meeting." She kept walking to nowhere.

"It'll only take a second." I said. She swung around and looked at a Gee like hurry up. "The Reminisce."

"What? What are you talking a...o' my God, is that you Joe?" I nodded my head yes real fast like she was about to give it up. "How can this be?" She laughed. "The reminisce huh'? Well a lot has changed since then." She started walking towards an office that I've already cleaned. I ran behind her like a poodle—just like I did ten years ago when she was the only one who wouldn't give a brotha' no play.

"What's changed, you still fine and well put together?" I said. She smiled and blushed a little but didn't say nothin'. "So you gon' answer me? I tried to be cool with my smile. "I see you still like to play hard to get. So you not gon' answer me? What, cat got cho' tongue?" I asked her while smilin' harder. She even smell good too.

49

"Actually alot." She dabbed at her forehead with a small piece of tissue. "I'm a changed woman."

"How, you already knew the Man Up-Stairs? You were the most Christian chick I ever met. Helped make a man out of me by not givin' me my way. Man, and I wanted some that night too." We smiled together as our imaginations took us back. "Those satin sheets didn't slide that night." She burst out laughin' like I'm some kinda' comedian.

"So how have life been treating you?" She said, trying to change the subject.

"Like a man in prison."

"That bad? You don't look like it. Well maybe by this job you have."

I turned and looked around, embarrassed by what she just said. "Awe' it's just a side somethin' for right now. Tryin' to turn my life around."

"I see you're still doing the trench coat thing?"

"Yea' that'll never change. That's just me baby. You ain't never had no problems wit' it."

"And I still don't. I'm glad you're trying to change your life." She stopped like she wanted to cut a tear. "I remember when I was saved and close to the Lord." (Hosea 11:7)

"Was?"

"Yep, was. I've gotten far a way from Him." (Jeremiah 3:14) She said. I cut a smile like here's my chance to get me some. "My life has done a 360 degree turn—you wouldn't believe it."

"I probably wouldn't. So what's up with you now?"

"I'm a legal secretary for P & P Attorneys at Law down the hall and I have a second job a night."

"What's yo' job at night Ms. Candy."

"O' I see you remember my name?"

"How could I forget. It means what it is." I winked at her.

"Awe' that's so sweet."

"Exactly." I winked again. She giggled as if to say, sweet but those are some tied lines.

"I'm an actress on the Hollywood stage." She laughed hard, but then got serious like she thought about it.

"So a actress huh'? Like what kind of acting? Romance?"

"Yea', something like that. You're invited if you'd like to come?"

"I can dig it. Where, when, and what time?" I took out some paper from the trench.

"At J.C. Acting Hall. Don't know the time right now. Just look it up in the phone book."

"I'm pretty popular and I know all of Bronx. Why I ain't never heard bout' this joint? And what's the name of the Hall?"

"Probably because it's private and they just opened it day before yesterday. And I just told you the name."

"So you can act like you in Hollywood huh'? Why I ain't never knew that?"

"Because you never tried to get to know me. Remember Mr. Reminisce? You left that night going after some Swishers and never came back. I think you ran from the Christian thang' or the fact that you couldn't get no play." She had the nerve to throw up two fingers like she was puttin' em' in quotes.

"That could be true. A man wasn't tryin' to get it on with Jesus, I wanted some from you."

"But you couldn't have me because that's who I was with." She made the woow' sound like I got cha'.

"Ok you got a brotha'! But what's up now? That was then, but this' now, Ms. 360 degree?"

She couldn't say nothin' for bout' a minute. Cat had her tongue real good. "Good seeing you again." She walked off like she owned this dirty joint, and was not waitin' for my words.

"Yea' like wise!" I tried to gather my words from lookin' at her beauty from behind in that two piece hot red dress suit. "Hey what's up with the phone number? And what's the name of the joint?" I tried yellin' again, but she never answered me, just disappeared goin' in the same ol' stanked up office I bet she came out of. "Man, that brawd's always been a challenge. I bet I win this time." I gave myself dap, grabbed the cleanin' equipment and bucket and left goin' to the car.

‎ℭ𝔰

I thought about Candy all the way back to the office. Can't wait to see this 360 degree Candy.

Ch. 4

Me, Cross, and some dudes he know are playin' some poker in one their abandoned houses they hide out in. Some of them are puttin' dime bags in for collateral, while Cross and me are just playin' for straight cash. I'm lettin' em' try and make their sale before dark. Cross is a crazy Cat. He just got some new powder so he wanna' show off and thangs. "Yo' man this' the works." He passed it to me. "That's some good stuff. Sniff it." I sniffed it. "How is it?"

"Gotta' money smell to it." We all laughed loud.

"That's what's up. Now taste the tip with your pinky." I closed my eyes, sighed, and smiled like I just tasted some candy. "Now, is that presidential or what?"

"That's more than presidential, know what I'm talkin' bout'?"

"I hear ya'." We slapped hands on into a quick one arm hug, with the release of a hand shake and the snapping of our fingers.

ೞ

Our laughs, cursin' each other out while tryin' to over power each other with words, came as the latest style for over five hours at the poker table. Now this wanna' be baller's tryin' to get me for my doe so I gotta' get em'. With all the commotion goin' on, I got up and shot him in the head from across the table as everybody's scattering for their own lives. Some are hiddin' behind furniture while others are hiddin' in the other rooms.

I shot him until my bullets said that's enough (*Genesis 9:5*). That's one thing about me, don't nobody play with my money. These fools don't understand who I am, so I'm lettin' em' know. I keeps my money on my mind and my mind on my money. Cross and the dudes except for the dead one said, find me. I walked out of the house like Mr. Eastwood in his best western movie. When I got out to the Benz, Cross was sittin' in the passenger seat as if he was the get-a-way man but in the wrong seat. I grinned to myself. Cross is lookin' scared— scared to say his own name. I got in the car, grabbed a big towel from the back, wipped off all the evidence, got back out, walked over to the gutter and threw it in as deep as I could. I'm thinkin' this' the norm, it ain't no thang. A thug ain't got no friends. May be friends one minute and the next worst enemies; especially when it comes to their money.

⋑⋐

I tried to turn my life around by gettin' a J.O.B., but it didn't work or did I really give it a try even though I haven't quit? I ask myself. Pricilla don' went all the way in with that church thang. Her lil' ol' girlfriend don' snatched her from me though. She don't even wanna' spend no time with me no mo', let alone give up the goods. Always too tired, or listenin' to her sanctimonious CD's when she's awake, or either sleep when I get to the crib late. Only thang' that's keepin' me here, is her cookin' and her cleanin'; and the fact that I'm still in love with her—what ever. My thoughts compiled me as I walked back to the Benzo and silently got in. I slowly glanced at Cross, I can feel his fear with his fingers wrapped around a nine. "Yo' man Cross, if you ever mess me around and turn on me, I'll kill you." I didn't crack a smile. "Now take yo' hand from around that gun cause' you'll never have the guts to blow me away. You too scared and stupid!" I raised my voice as if to be talkin' to a lil' ol' boy. He's sweatin' like a hostage with a gun to his head. "Are you that scared of me that you would shoot me Cross? Huh'?" He didn't open up his mouth, he just knodded his head 'yes' real fast. I reached over and snatched the gun out of his hand with no fear. He jumped like a lil' girl. "Man you too weak to roll wit' me! What up with you!?"

"Yo' man, I'm scared. You ain't never loaded off like that on nobody befo'."

"What?"

"Normally it only take about two shots."

"It took too many to take care of business. Say man get out of my car you actin' too soft. What happened to you? Thought you was a hard Gee? Somebody don' rolled yo' pants down and bent chu' over?!" I laughed as loud as I could and helped him get out of the car with my fist, and sped down the street.

ᎧᏕ

I almost felt like that was the last time I'm gon' see my homey Cross again. He just gave up oughta' nowhere, til' he called me on my cell two hours later beggn' for forgiveness like a brawd I just broke up with. "Cross man you ain't gotta' do all that." My line beeped. I looked at the light blue highlight of the front of my cell. It's Pricilla, I cracked a smile. She's my princes. "Hey Cross it's cool, let me hit chu' back—Hey got somethin' goin' down later on when dawn breaks, you wanna' roll?"

"Yea' man, that's cool." He got happy.

"Cool. I'll hit chu' back." I hung up and answered the other line. "Yo' what up sweetness?"

"O' so I'm sweet now huh'?"

"You always sweet."

"What ever, you must want some?"

"That would help."

"Help what?"

"Help calm a man's nerves."

"Come on." She whispered.

"Come on where?" I got excited and sped up goin' in and out of traffic. I can't believe what I just heard.

"Come on over here."

"I'm on my way!" I got so happy I almost punched my speedometer to the limit. When I got home and stepped foot into the front living room, she was already prepared, waitin' on my words—and I couldn't wait to give em' to her. "Pricilla we ain't done this since you been all wrapped up with the church thang. You sure this ain't a set up and a bunch of church women ain't gon' jump out of the closet, and do a revival on me while splashin' oil and layin' their greasy hands all over me?" We laughed real sweet to keep the mood. I can't believe I'm nervous. A thug like me ain't never been nervous of no woman. Maybe it got somethin' to do with about two years ago when the Man Up-Stairs came on the scene. I now know she loves Him, and I wouldn't be mad if she fall and give it to me.

ଔ

I could barely get the bedroom door open as she walked up to me with this sparklin' red gee-string teddy and my favorite red pumps on. She quickly unbuttoned my button-down as we quickly made our way over and stood in front of the bed. She made her way all around, and on down until all of my

59

buttons and zippa's are nowhere to be found. I sighed and huffed at her touch that I had been longin' for. I sat down on the edge of the bed as my dark chocolate body is now exposed. I'm sayin' to myself, somethin's different but it feels too good to let go. She kept doin' her thang' as I watched and caressed the back of her neck. "I just wanna' please you." She whispered.

I turned away as she rolled her fingernails slowly down my back—which made me shiver. Somethin' happened when she said that. The mood changed from lust and passion *(Romans 12:1)* to conviction. That same flash back from two years ago just flashed befo' my eyes again. I jumped up. She kept tryin' to kiss me. "Stop." I forced the words out as my desire forced to push em' back in. "Stop Pricilla. Stop. You don't have to do this." I tried movin' away. Even though I'm all man, and a man never turns down a woman's touch and readiness to fulfill. I just can't let her do this. "Baby, I said stop." I gently grabbed her head with my hand and started caressing her hair as I slowly pulled away. "You don't have to do this." Our whispers are our conversation.

"But I want to. I just wanna' please you. I don't want you to leave me." A tear rolled from her eyes.

I pulled her up and held her. I knew I felt somethin' different. "Pricilla I love you no matter what. Don't get me wrong I want this, but I feel bad cause' I know you tryin' to do the right thang'—readin' the bible and goin' to church, and I feel bad cause' I'm the cause of your fall." *(1 Thessalonians 4:3)* She burst out crying and laid back against the cream colored comforter and balled up like a baby.

"Lord I'm so sorry. It's hard to keep myself, I'm tryin' so hard." She cried out like The Man Up Stairs is standin' right in front of us. Fear came over me. "Joe I'm so in love with you, I just wish that we could get married and all of this would be right."

I slowly slid off the bed, stood up, and went to the dresser where I always keep my jewelry. "We can't get married right now. It ain't a good time for me right now. Got too much ridin'. Got way too many mouth's to feed with my white powdered packages. I'm makin' too much, I'm right where I wanna' be." She raised up from the side of the bed as I walked back over to her and wrapped my arms around her lower waist with her head thrusted into my chest. "Look Pricilla if we get married now, it'll mess things up. It's not the right time. Plus I just started working too."

"You know…" She ignored my job thang and began talkin' as the tears started rollin' down her face. "…God is really dealing with me. I've never been where I'm at with Him like I am right now. I wanted so badly to please you because I knew you were gettin' tired of my new faith. And I figured if I just give myself to you, you won't go nowhere. It's a struggle for me just like it is for you. It's harder for me because I have an image to uphold for you, my new church family, and God. The fact that we weren't saved before I gave my life back to God has made it harder for me *(James 1:14).* I'm scared. I feel like I have to choose. Baby you all I know. And you the only one who knows how to make me feel special, but if I can make you realize you are as special as you make me feel, your special can't even touch the special that God makes me feel."

I pulled away and stood up. Jealousy's written all over my face. Almost to a point that I hate this God she talkin' bout'. He don' changed my lady's attitude and mind-set about the way she feels about me. Her Chief. Can't no man out do me. I'm the man. "Ain't nobody greater than me." I pointed to myself. "I'm the only one who knows where yo' spot is. I'm the only one who knows where to touch you at. I'm the only one who knows how to take you on a roller coaster ride. I'm the only one who knows how to make you feel special like that—I'm the one!" I patted my chest which turned into hard pounds. I raised my voice with pride, rage, and anger as I kept pointing to myself.

"See Joe you don't get it, you namin' all the things that you can do on the out side, but I'm talking about what he does to me on the inside. And what God does on the inside for me, is what lasts."

I'm so mad I can burst her in her face. "So why you call me over here then! And why you had to have me instead of this GOD you talkin' bout'? Why He couldn't fulfill your desires?

I'm just on the outside, remember?" I walked to the room door too ready to leave.

She turned me around with her yellin' words. "Because I'm a fool in love with a man that I know is not good for me right now! And the fact that I don't wanna' loose you!" Tears ran from her eyes. "I can't even see myself watchin' you with no other chick wrapped around yo' arms!" She yelled and came rushin' up to me as if she was gon' hit me. I jumped back like a gal—surprised. "The women at the church was right!"

"Thea' you go with that church crap!"

"I knew I should've listened to them instead of calling you over here trying to please something that only God can please! Change something only God can change!" She yelled with more tears falling from her eyes. Her voice trembled. I know she mad. "They said if a man try to size himself up with God, he is a dangerous man and that I needed to get away from him, and I'm starting to see all that right now! Joe I don't know what makes you think that you can size up to GOD!" She yelled as she threw both of her hands in the air waggin' her fingers as if the make a quote. "GOD will make you bow down one way or the other!" *(Romans 14:11)*

"You ain't scarin' nobody! Woman I'm outha'..." I ran up to her and raised my hand to slap her but her words threw my hand back into a weak balled up fist. I know there's a Greater Force with her.

63

"If you hit me I guarantee you, you won't get away with it!" She said as my balled up fist turned into a sweaty palm. I know she talkin' bout' the Man Up-Stairs.

"Man I'm oughta' here, I ain't got no time to hear bout' somethin' that ain't makin' me no livin'. You can be confused all by yo'self foolin' with all those church hypocrites. They fixin' they mouths tryin' to tell you right when they all layin' under somebody! Ever since you met this so-called sanctimonious friend, I knew she wasn't gon' be nothin' but trouble! Gone then, gone and join her and look like some kinda' cult group! What chall' do, get together and drink blood (*Micah 5:12)?!*"

"Get out of my house you devil! Satan the Lord rebuke you (*Zechariah 3:2)!*" I started laughin'. "The Blood of Jesus is against you! I said it before, and I'm saying it again, Joe you better choose God or you won't be here long! That gangsta'-fied, thugish fire you playin' with ain't gon' last long! And when your back is truly up against the wall, either you gon' run to the Lord or you gon' run to the devil. You think you the man with all that pride and can't nothing and nobody beat you, and ain't nobody stronger than you, I'm here to tell you Joe it will all come crashin' down!"

I stepped outside the door like what ever—I mean what I say. She slammed the door in my face like she heard my thoughts. I walked off, lit a Black & Myles laughin'; and sayin' to myself, "she may've put a lil' fear in a thug's heart, but it ain't enough to stop what I got poppin' right now." I whispered a little bit, but not enough for her to hear me. I took the straps of my trench coat, tied it tight around me, and walked off goin' to the Benz thinkin', I know she still love me and I know she ain't goin' nowhere. I'll let her cool off, she'll hit me back later.

Ch. 5

J ust got a call on my cell by a familiar number. I programmed her name in my phone. Candy big as day showed up. My horizon went up in the air. Pricilla ain't givin' me no play, maybe Ms. Candy will. I called the number back only to notice that it's a teller marketer beggin' for some money. I wonder how in the world I got her number programmed in my cell? Must've been dreamin' cause' she never gave me her number. She got me thinkin' hard about her. I'm still tryin' to cope with this feeling she put on me. Got my mind changin' thoughts every minute, but yet, got the nerve to be interrupted by thoughts of Pricilla too and the fact of her movin' out. Thoughts from Pricilla to Candy, Candy to Pricilla. Bring back memories of an old love song Candy Girl. Candy girl you are my world, I need your love each and everyday…and on and on and on. I laughed out loud. That ol' timin' stuff ain't gon' cut it with the situation I'm in. Pricilla ain't even called me. I went home one night and her stuff said find me. This Jesus stuff is really taken her to another planet, and believe it or not, she ain't given in. I seen times when all I had to do is take my trench off, unroll the duffel bag, show her a lil' powder, and she was all mine. But now I'm gon' have to work a lil' harder. I see I'm workin' with a Higher Power that's a Gee Himself and a Thug's challenge. Ain't nobody ever touched my lady's heart like me. This must be some kinda' Strong Force. I just got one question to ask anybody who would have the nerve to come in my face and say that this' real. I'd ask em' how can a person love this Thing that Pricilla call God, that they can't even see *(1 John 4: 7-21)*? And how can a person feel this God, that don't have no arms or legs *(John 4: 24, Ezekiel 36: 27)*? Somebody better have some mind changin' answers. Until then, my mind's made up, I don't believe in Him *(Isaiah 44:6,24, 45:18-23)*. Can't nothin' and nobody change that.

∛

The roads got the nerve to be slippery from the rain. Been rainin' a lot lately like somebody prayed for it. Cross and nem' got somethin' rollin' at his crib, I think a pool party. Got some honey's there to keep us company. Nice entertainment ain't half bad with the right kind of entertainment.

I pulled up on the wet grass in the front yard cause' all the cars had all the drive-way space. It's packed out, the beat of gangsta' rap is shakin' the ground. Cross just bought him an old seventy's style, wooden floor, ol' and ghetto' lookin'

Victorian styled home; and got the nerve to have a small pool in the back yard. Music's poppin' from the outside to the latest jam. One thing about Cross, that fool know how to put a party together. Anybody would think he's puttin' his own bachelor party together by the looks of thangs.

I walked in. The honeys are everywhere with their spray of different bikini's and tight fittin' clothes on. Some got the nerve to slide down the pole and finger toward my direction to come and join em'. Cross burst out laughin' like he'd been waitin' for me to arrive about half the day. Everybody's showin' plenty of love, givin' me plenty of dap into quick hugs. Cross was the first. Popularity has always been on my side. I think they're just glad that I came back. I lost a lot of respect when I got a 9 to 5. All of these Cats got their own jobs and they ain't 9 to 5's. We all entrepreneurs to be reckoned with. We the ghetto Corporate American gangsta' thug style. It's funny how women think. They all over a Gee when they find out you got some money and got cho' own stuff. But right when yo' cash say find me? They say find me.

℞

The party went on for what seem like hours. My world's spinnin' right now. I'm loaded with nothin' but weed, coke and liquior. Man I love smokin' me some weed. A nice big fat blunt does a body good.

This fine shorty bout' 5'0 ft. with a gee-string got the nerve to come up and holla'. "Hey you, I see you set right for the occasion." She said, like she know I'm high.

I looked down at her. "Yea' I'm feelin' real good right about now."

She tiptoed to talk to me. "I see. Can I be a part of what you're feelin'?"

"It depends."

"Depends on what?"

"Depends on what you about to come wit'."

"Well first of all, can I say that I'm really diggin' you?"

"O' really? That's what's up."

"As many guy's as it is up in here right about now, you're the only one I'm payin' attention to."

"Straight?"

"Straight."

"Well you know we can go somewhere where we can hear each other better over the loud music. Follow me to the back of the house." I yelled over the music as I looked down at her for her approval.

"I'm right behind you." She followed me like a lil' puppy wantin' its treat. I got her right where I want her and didn't even have to work for it. She must got somethin'. This' way too easy to get. I ain't gon' sleep with this one I think she got somethin'. I turned around. "What's up, you changed your mind?" She asked with a slight frown.

"Yep'. I'm hangin' wit' my boy Cross. Just wanna' chill, can I take a rain check?"

I ran up on her and rubbed her sensitive spot. She hurried up and said, "yes". She went her way and I went mine knowin' that I'd never get wit' no beggin' woman. I likes me a challenge. When they too easy, you gotta' wonder what they got. Probably Crabs or the Claps, or a bacteria infection.

೮೩

The party lasted what seemed like forever. Everybody danced til' the sun came up. Cross and I didn't cross paths too much. I'm cool with that cause' I know what it take to pull off a good party. You gotta' watch everybody and yo' liquor. Make sure everything stay regulated and don't get out of control.

"Yo' Cross, yo' man I'm out. Everything was on point. Hey man, next time tighten up on the Honey's you invite." He laughed like he thought about what I said to be true as one of them walked by in a pink two piece bikini with brown cowboy boots on. We both just shook our heads and laughed again.

"Next time I'll be sure to work on that." We both laughed again as another homely lookin' chick walked by. Cross just shook his head again and said, "I blew this one."

I reiterated the comment. "Yea' bro' you sho' did." I laughed again but stopped cause Cross' feelings is starten' to show that he want some peppin' up talk, like how the party was good and all; which makes it hard cause' I don't agree. It was arite. "Cross, yo' man this party was on point."

"Yo' man for real?" He answered quick like he was waiting for that.

Cross looks up to me. All the young Cat's look up to me. I don't like to be looked up to. I'm not a good roll model. My life ain't no play toy. I'm in some real stuff and shouldn't no Cat be lookin' up to me. "Yea' man can't wait til' the next one. I'm out."

"Arite." He walked me out to the Benz. "What's up, you ain't been out with us in decades? You out later on tonight?" Cross looked hopin' I'd agree.

"Man you know I'm out of the game." I said.

"Game ain't over til' the fat lady sang." He said.

"She been sang." He looked funny and I looked serious but no words transpired. I jumped in the Benz, backed up and burned off down the road to nowhere, thinkin' bout' changin' my mind.

Ch. 6

I 'm runnin' for my life again. Sweats pourin' down the side of my temples. I've gotten myself in this thang way too deep—again. Pricilla may be mad at me right now but I know she would kill me if she found out that I was involved in the game again after I decided not to. I knew this' what Cross wanted. Two of the fella's and Cross are down, last time I saw em', they were layin' across each other, wounded from a spray of bullets. We all got sprayed but unfortunately I'm the one that didn't get hit. I say unfortunately cause' if they're dead, I'd rather be where they are. I'm still runnin'. My life is too much pain—the pain of cold hearted reality of gettin' nowhere. The pain of livin' in hiding rather than livin' free. Gotta' watch my back every step I take, every move I make. It's the thug life I know, and I'm trapped in it like a sucka' with the wrapper over it. Again, nobody could care less whether I died today or tomorrow. The thought of me gettin' out of the game came a long time ago. I knew I couldn't, cause' a thug just don't get out of the game. But they say God loves thugs too. So if He so real He'll get me out again. I'm startin' to think different bout' Em'. Just maybe I might be on His mind somewhere in that Place in the sky. I think it's called Heaven. I ask myself, out of all I've been through, I wonder if He would give up on a Cat like me *(Hebrews 13:5)?* They say He ain't like the world. The Man above accepts us thugs just the way we are. I skidded around the corner of the abandoned, brick, warehouse building with my steel toe boots so fast that I split a hole on the side, from my pinkie toe to the top of my ankle. The cops are drawing near. I can hear the sound of the sirens buzzin' through my eardrums like a hummin' bee on a bee hive. I'm runnin' out of my shoes I can't get caught. The thoughts of Pricilla ran through my mind. She made me promise that I would get out of the game. Of course that promise came while she was takin' care of my needs. Maybe that's why I said yes. She knows I didn't mean it. It's almost impossible to get out of the thug life. The only way any thug can get out, is like I said before, "The Man Above." Feel like I'm runnin' to nowhere. I jumped inside of this huge, big round broken sewage pipe in the ground that's missing its lid as it came into my view. Before I realized that it was full of, for lack of better words, stanky mess, I threw up without hesitation. I almost passed out as I heard feet runnin' over my head but never invading my hidin' place. They're determined to find me, and I'm determined not to get caught. After this I promise I'm gon' become a believer. I'm confused. All I can hear in my brain is Pricilla's preachin'. Man I promise I'll listen to her for now on. I'm still in love with that woman. I can see a vision of her sayin': "You better choose Christ, or you won't be here long." It meant nothin' to me then cause' I was still doin' my own thang, but now it means my life and freedom. Sweat's pourin' down my face. The chance of freedom got me wonderin'. I can say goodbye to the lil' ol' janitorial job I just got. Cross would be happy, but I let him talk me into goin' out for the last time. It's the last time alright. Now I don't know if he's dead or alive. The chances of me findin' that out is almost none. I don't know if I'll make it out of this stank hole alive or not. I hear voices, some far away and some near—so near seem like they can whisper in my ear.

ଔ

Night came and went like the color of black and white. I looked up from about eight feet down and saw a mist of sun light from the lid of the man hole suage tank. All of the voices have disappeared. I'm still stuck in stanky mess, too scared to move. Feel like they may be standin' right beside the hole waitin' on me to come out with my hands up. My brain went dead and my eyes went black. I can't say how long I've been inside this hole. Probably been only a day until all the heat cooled off. I moved my arms to see if they still worked. They do. Now I'm slightly movin' my legs to see if they still work too. They do. I'll never let Cross talk me into doin' this again. I only did it to please him and the boy's cause' they had a problem with me gettin' a nine to five. I should've followed my first mind. My first mind told me to stay in the house and go spend time with Pricilla, but no that other mind which I now know wasn't the right mind told me to go kick it wth my boys and make them happy. Wrong choice. It's crazy cause' all of the man holes I know don't have mess in it, somebody must of took a leak and messed all night in this thing. I gotta' get oughta' here. I slowly moved my arm's up to grab a hold of the cemented latter to pull myself up. My legs slowly followed as my arms did the leadin'. As I got to the top, I tilted my head back until only my eyes could see the lining of what looked like a brick building. I know they gone. I slowly and with all the care in the world pulled myself to the top only to fall back inside cause' a rat just ran across my forehead. I tried it again, this time gettin' all the way out, dirty and stanky. My trench looks like a black wrinkled up raincoat. I don't even care, look like I'm a free man again. I tried crackin' a smile, but if I did, the bad boys would run from around the corner and grab me and take me off to the pen.

cs

Come to find out all the dudes that was with Cross and me never made it out alive. One of my boys from around the projects came and told me after I called em' on the hush hush after things cooled off. They said it was all on the news. A big mess is what they called it. The flash back of all those bodies I saw when I looked back as I ran for my life makes me quiver. All of em' lyin' across each other was all dead bodies, even Crosses. This' a day that I'll never forget. This' what the game will get cha'. The wounds was too great. Like stickin' a band-aide on a gun shot wound. My boy got oughta' here. I hope the Man Upstairs let em' in. I know he's done a lot wrong that would make the Man Upstairs say no. But hopefully that won't be the case when he get there. Man I miss Cross. He was my right hand man. I could count on him to carry my stuff and to take care of important business, even though he was a lil' ol' scared chicken. I gotta' crack a smile to old memories.

ꞯ

Crosses funeral was over like somebody flicked a lighter but the lighter wouldn't come on. It was like nobody even had time to mourn for him. The preacher act like he didn't even know Cross. I guess cause' he didn't give him those dividends every Sunday. Church ain't nothin' but a money makin' thang'. Every preacher over a church get off on makin' bigger churches and havin' packed out congregations. And half of em' don't even care bout' non of em'. I can say this cause' I was one of them. Talked bad about a Gee. All I can remember is that I started to pull my nine out and shoot all of em' but Cross and nem' held me back with their words. I ain't been back since. This' the first time in years since I laid foot on a church yard and I ain't makin' it no habit. Everybody packed Crosses funeral out and when the preacher got up to do his so-called thang', everybody who knew they wasn't livin' right, flew out the church. *(2 Corinthians 5:8) (Matthew 7:21)* The greatest Thugs in town were there. All the projects were packed in that lil' ol' temple which reminded me of a lil' church on the prairie. Everybody was gee'd up, lookin' their best; sharper than the sharpest needle. All the fine chicks and even their's were fine—old as they were. I can tell some of em' were well taken care of. It was a, if you take care of me, I'll take care of you kinda' thang'. Boy the thug life is a trip.

❧

Come to find out one of the brawds that used to be one of my call girls came to Crosses funeral and dropped the low down on a Gee. Two low downs in one. Cross, now this. I'm too swift and too cool to find out that I got an eight year old son. I'm already fightin' for my rights, blood test, and whatever else. I gotta' make sure this lil' Gee is really mine. Women lie so much. They'll lie just to get my last dime. I admit she was a regular, but I made sure she was on the pill. She went every month and got her a new set. Must've tricked me when I started trusting her and lettin' her go by herself as long as she kept givin' it up.

She walked him over to me with her hand on top of his head. "Say hey to yo' daddy."

"Hey." He flashed a quick hand up in the air and looked down as if the ground was me.

I ought not say nothin' cause' she probably lyin'. "What up lil' Gee? I don't know bout' bein' yo' Pops, but you can still give me some dap." I said. He's nervous, I can tell cause' he bald up his fist and dropped it on top of mine like a whimp. I see he been around his Moms way too much. My Lil' Gee ain't gon' have no suga' in his lil' tank. I see I gotta' toughin' em' up.

"That's all you gon' say? What up lil' Gee?" She pushed him towards me.

"That's all I need to say. I'll get wit' you later on this subject. Now is not a good time."

I tried walking away but she stepped up with a loud voice. "O' it's a good time alright!" She raised her voice so loud, everybody turned their head lookin' scared.

Somehow in the back of my mind I knew this situation would come up in my life. "Look woman you better leave while you got the chance cause' case you didn't know, I beat up women who step to me like a man."

"You ain't gon' do nothin'!" She waved her hand in my face. The lil' whimp tried to hold her back like her lil' man. "All you need to do is tell me how you gon' take care of yo' child?"

"Look woman I'm a tell you one mo' time to get back before I give you somethin' to yell about." Some of the women who had been layin' eyes on me earlier walked away disappointed

79

while others are still lookin' on as if to wanna' see a show down. I'm bout' to give em' something to see.

Some of the attendants ran over and told her to leave. She tried puttin' up a good fight. I'm kinda' glad they did cause' it kept me from layin' her out.

ଔ

I never got a chance to see if the whimp was really mine. If she had of came at me right like a solid, professional woman, I'd a given her what she wanted—a test to see if that lil' dude was really my mini me eventhough he looks nothin' like me.

The streets are dead. Nobody in sight. I can't get Cross off my mind. I miss the ol' Gee. I don't know how I'm gon' make it without em'. I pulled the Benz over and gave em' my respect for bout' 30 minutes with thoughts and some small tears.

Ch. 7

The light on my cell lit up under the covers. Say's Kizzy's Janitorial Service. Thought they fired me by now, it's been weeks. I rolled over. My cell blew up again. "Man I ain't tryin' to hear that right now. Got a good sleep goin' on and got the nerve to call a brotha' at 5:30 in the mornin'. I ain't tryin' to hear that." I mumbled to the chick I just met at the grocery store. Don't even know her name just saw her, struck up a conversation, took her by the hand, and brought her home with me. She was good conversation and a warm body to lay on—that's all. Now it's time for her to go. Got my pleasure, now I'm satisfied. Had to see what was underneath all that spandex and thin halter-top she was wearin'. The thought of Candy's beautiful, fine, silhouette of her body just flashed before my eyes. The unbearable thought of what she look like exposed, had me to answer the phone on the eighth ring. "What up, dis' Joe?"

"What up?" She sarcastically repeated me.

"Say what chu' gotta' say."

"I will when you learn how to answer the telephone." She snickered to herself. I'm sayin' to myself, I'm bout' to put her on blast if she say one more crazy word. "This is Kizzy's..."

I had to cut her off. "I know who you are. The white chick that ain't never liked me since the first time I set foot in that midget of an office called Kizzy's Janitorial Service. One foot in, and one foot out." She didn't laugh but I did.

"Very unprofessional. Anyway, Boss Man, as you call him, when you should call him by his name: Mr. Kizzy, which would sound so much better. He wants you to come in today. Are you available, even though you haven't been here in weeks?"

"Of course not. Ya'll know I ain't available. Talkin' that non sense."

"Actually you really don't have a choice. Either come in today or do not come back anymore. I personally think he's giving you too many chances anyway." She had the nerve to say.

"You make me sick."

"Well, you're not the first one, and I'm sure you will not be the last one."

I'm thinkin', I need to go cause' I can use the cash since I ain't runnin' the streets full time no mo'. "Tell Boss Man I'm on my way."

"Sure, no problem. I knew you wouldn't disagree."

I hung up in her face.

 C8

As soon as I kicked the brawd out, I started throwin' on my tied ol' uniform.

C8

Rollin' down the big Avenue brings back memories. Pusher's and prostitute's got their corners bright and early on this dark, damp cool mornin' with the dew on the grass and all. Wanna' complain but I ain't cause' it don't do no good no way. Drops of rain scattered themselves across my windshield like at any moment they gon' turn into a lil' ol' rain storm. That ain't gon' stop the pushers and the prostitutes. They work day and night, rain', sleet, shine, or snow.

The sign Kizzy's Janitorial Service blurred in the short distance from the pickup of the rain. This' crazy, I ain't even got no umbrella. The trench has always been enough for me even though it ain't got no hood. Kinda' my trademark. If you see the trench, you see me, no matter what kind of weather it is. This time it's a lil' different. I think its gon' be too much rain for me to handle. I'll make a run for it when I get out.

C8

As soon as I walked through the glass doors, Boss Man couldn't wait to give me orders and the first degree; and Ms. Big Mouth couldn't wait to start naggin'. Throwing the rain water off of my trench were my come back words.

This gee'd up nerd in a hot orange suit and mix matchin' tie got the nerve to be sittin' in the same seats I was sittin' in when I first set foot in this joint. Got his tooth pick legs crossed like he's waitin' to hear from the CEO in a big time executive office.

Boss Man left me and walked over to ol' boy and stuck out his hand like he didn't see me come in all wet up and thangs'. "I'm so glad you could interview with us this morning. I must admit, it was an excellent interview."

Ol' boy never stood up but met his hand with a hand shake—all off rhythm. "Like wise. I'm excited to see what this company has to offer." He smiled and I burst out laughin', turnin' all heads towards me.

Boss Man turned around like he didn't see me come in earlier or give me the first degree a few minutes ago. "O' Joe, I'm glad you could make it." I'm trippin', where's his memory? I barely smiled unnoticeable. "Hey I need you to train, David?" He turned and looked at ol' boy.

"Yes, David is my name." He sarcastically snickered to himself, raising one hand to his mouth as if to laugh prideful at Boss Man forgetting his name.

Boss Man waved his hand in my direction as if to brush me off. "David meet Joe Quick, Joe meet the best business man Kizzy's will ever have." He laughed so loud my ears rung and my attitude started burnin'. Shoot man, I'm the best; the best that will ever put up with this dirty unprofessional trash pit.

David jumped to his feet. "Um' yes sir, David, David Whitmore is my name." He stuck his hand out to shake mine but I didn't budge. He sat back down fast as if to be a lil' scared. This dude got the nerve to act like some nerd from a big time corporate American company. What he want with this joint? I hate to tell em', but he's in for a rude awakenin'.

"Joe I need you to train David." I laughed at Boss Man cause' he got a habit of repeatin' himself. Boss Man looked at the nerd. "He's going to be going out with you and you are to show him everything you know." Like whatever that is. Boss Man grinned like a Cheshire Cat jumped in him. I had to grin at that thought.

"That's cool." I shook some more of the rain water from my trench again.

"That's cool?" David asked, looking at Boss man like he should put me in check, but he couldn't cause' he talk like that sometimes himself.

Boss Man frowned at me like I had offended him. "Joe, like I said you're going to train David." Boss Man tried to smile at David like he's tryin' to make him forget what I just said, "...and you're going to take him out on your runs and you will train him on everything you know." He said, repeating himself again. I'm thinkin'. I don't know nothin'. "You and David will work close until he's confident to clean on his own." Boss Man reached to shake this Cats hand for bout' the thousandth time. I guess I should start callin' em' both by their names. Mr. Kizzy and David. Man that's soft. Sounds too soft for a thug like me. I'll stick with Boss Man and I'll think of another name for this chump, David—Nerd. "No problem Boss Man, got em' covered." I walked up to the counter to get my runs.

Ms. Attitude had to open up her mouth. "I sure hope you do not turn this nice guy into your rough, ghetto project image, and horrible attitude."

I fired up a Black & Mild and went around the counter and blew it in her face. "I was waitin' on you." She started choking. "Is that a horrible enough attitude for you Ms. Big Mouth?" The Nerd's eye's got big like he just seen a ghost. Probably thought I was gon' slap her.

She finally stopped choking. "I hope you get fired for lighting that gangster stick up in this business." She turned and looked at Boss Man, waiting on his response but he walked back into his office like he didn't see nothin'. I laughed and took another puff and put it out on her name tag that's sittin' on the counter. I was tryin' to do right but people will make you stay doin' wrong *(Romans 7: 7-24)*.

Boss Man came back out when all the commotion settled down. He walked over to David and shook his hand once again. "Ok David, I'm excited to have you on board with us. With your ten year experience in corporate America, you'll enjoy working with us, we're the best business in America!" Boss Man looked at me daring me to say a word or he was gon' fire me. I know its cause' he know he's lyin'.

"Yo' man David let's go." I grabbed the clip board with all of the lists of appointments on them from off the counter. David followed me like I'm the one that hired him. This might be easier than I think.

ᘓ

David couldn't wait to get back to the car and start firing up at the mouth. I couldn't shut him up if I offered him all the money in the world.

"So Joe. Is it Joe?" I just stared at em' like my gangster look was his yes. His voice started tremblin'. "Your name is Joe right? I don't want to call you out of your name. I like the name Joe...It's very becoming of you." He said shaking.

Now I'm lookin' over at em' like shut up I ain't gon' hurt chu'. "Yea' chief, Joe's my name."

"Chief?"

I couldn't help but laugh at his corny personality. "Yea' Chief. That means you da' man." He smiled like that comforted him. This Cat looks just like the craziest nerd people see on the tube. He's the nerdiest black Cat I've ever seen in my life. He got this big uncombed fro that's been out of style since the 70's. It's funny cause' I can pimp the suit he's wearin' with the unmatchin' under shirt and tie and the bifocal glasses taped up in the middle and on each end just to keep em' together. He trips me out with his five foot seven puny stature. If you blow at em' he'll fall over at any given moment. Kinda' feel sorry for the wanna' be Gee, got pimples all over his face like he took a pill to make em' grow. I know he feel ugly, probably why he's nerdy. It's a trip cause' as nerdy as he looks, he's as smart as a dictionary. Never know what people don' been through to make em' act, look, and be the way they are. I'm a thug but I'm not dumb. It's just my style. I consider myself a very smart, intelligent, and GQ Cat. I like saggin' pants, a blingin' gold grill, steel toe boots; might even wear the latest gears on my feet. When I dress up, I might even put me on some jeans, a white button down, a blazer with my trench over it, and an all-white matchin' baseball cap, as white as a dove. That's my way of dressin' up and lookin' ready for the ladies.

This Cat won't shut up for nothin'. His loud squawky voice is annoying to my thoughts. "So um' Chief." I burst out laughin' again. He cheesed real hard showin' all of his 32 yellow grill. "Um', so how long have you been working for this corporation?"

"You think this joint is a corp.?" I burst out laughin'. "Yo' man you sho' in the wrong place. This ain't close to bein' no corporation." We put all the cleanin' stuff in the trunk and took off down the street.

"Well Mr. Kizzy said that this was a Corporation in the making."

"Man how you think this is a corporation in the roughest side of downtown Bronx? Leakin' ceiling and stanked up carpet, old as mathusa'. The sheetrock on the walls is peelin' off and don' turned colors. This ain't the corp. you thank this is."

"I was thinking more on the lines of now since we have the credentials, and looks like the books are kept, and the stock markets on the rise for this type of business…"

"Look Geek, I mean Dav' man, you sound like some kinda' brain machine. Where'd you get cho' smarts from?"

"Through much studying."

"You had to do more than just study to be smart like that?"

"Studying brings intelligence, intelligence brings knowledge, knowledge brings wealth."

"Ok ok, you can drop it. I hate I said you was so smart cause' you takin' it way too far." Things got quiet like his feelings got hurt. Seem real fragile like he been hurt growin' up. I just looked at em' waitin' for him to pop out of it cause' I ain't his daddy and I sho' ain't his counselor.

"So Joe, where are you from?"

"South Bronx."

"I bet that's a beautiful place."

I eyed em' cause' he know he lyin'. "What chu' think?" He didn't answer for his own good. I know he's scared of me. Must be the trench. Pricilla used to say it made me look like a gangsta'. Which I don't know how a trench gon' make somebody look like a gangsta'? I still ask myself.

"Well if you must ask where I'm from." He said.

"I didn't."

"Well, I'll offer." I looked at em crazy like he's a bold lil' somethin'. "I'm from San Fransisco. Wow, I sure miss walking that Golden Gate Bridge."

"Yo' man, you walked all the way across that Bridge? Man do you know how far that is? What were you thinkin'?" He laughed at me like I'm some kinda' comedian. Dingy dude.

"No!" He slapped my shoulder. I looked at em' again like he was crazy. "I used to ride my scooter across it. That's much easier!" He burst out laughin' like some geek fool. I had to laugh a little cause' it was just that corney. "You should try something like that."

"Naw' Cat, I'll stick to watchin' ol' gal holdin' the torch at night."

"O' yea' the Statue of Liberty." He hugged himself. "She's so beautiful. Too bad she's just a statue." That fool had the nerve to sigh like he ain't never had none.

I grabbed the clip board from the side of the seat, slowed this jacked-up Escort down to a stop on the side of the road, and rolled the sheets over to the easiest job before lunch. "I'm bout' to show you how much of a corporation this joint is."

"What do you mean?" He looked at the sheets rolled back on the clip board.

"Wait til' we get where we goin'."

"I'm excited!"

"You won't be when we get there." I spun out like this ride has a turbo engine. Geek didn't say a word. I see I'm gon' have to fix him up with one of my left over ladies. I dug in my trench for a smoke.

⊂8

The parking lot is packed as usual. These some dedicated business people. I picked the worst buildin' to clean on purpose. Lil' D' need some initiation. I'm fixin' to make him out of a real man. He didn't do nothin' the last place we went.

We got out, I popped the trunk, and grabbed all the cleanin' stuff. Which ain't nothin' but a bucket, two mops, one broom, and some liquid detergent. Boss Man oughta' be a shame of his lazy cheap self.

⊂8

As soon as we walked in the building, walked over to the nearest restroom, Lil' D' held his nose and ran back outside and threw up all over the side walk. I walked back out real slow, fired up a smoke, laughed, took two puffs, flicked the smoke across the side walk, and walked back in pissed cause' this Geek is too soft. He ain't gon' make it.

I shoved the mop into the nasty mop water mad at the world. Thinkin'. Thinkin' bout' why I'm workin' for Uncle Tom, when I could be makin' straight cash everyday instead of every two weeks. Can't call the shots. All the shots belong to Boss Man, and somebody callin' em' over him. Everybody got somebody to answer too. But when I was livin' the thug life, I had it made. Had everybody answerin' to me. Pricilla was one of em'. I don't know what to say about that woman now. Ain't heard from her in weeks. I would've heard from her by now cause' it's right before her fertile time. One time we almost thought her fertile brought a lil' Gee, but came up a raw deal. Normally at that time she used to make a Gee real happy. Didn't have to beg or act nice, or sit up and bring her somethin' to eat, or rub her where she couldn't resist. The thought of it brought back memories only a man would have a wet dream from.

ᙯ

3 hours have passed with five offices, three restrooms, and a long hallway knocked out, with one last office to finish. Still no sign of Lil' D'. Think he gave up and quit. I knew he wouldn't last. Oop's spoke too soon. He just burst through the door like superman cheesin' with all of those thirty two yellow teeth just like I just started. "Ok I'm ready, let's clean this place!"

I could fall out. This Cat got the nerve to roll up in here with a torn bed sheet wrapped around his face. Crazy! "Fool, where you goin' with that? And where you been? Now do you believe this ain't no corporation?"

"O' yes sir, I'm a believer now. Is there still room for me?"

I looked around to find what don't need to be clean—which ain't nothin'. Everything is included. "Yo' man, go change that trash." I know he don't want to but he went, shakin' like a lil' ol' gal the whole time.

ᙯ

The weather can't make up its mind about what it wants to do. Wanna' be cold in this early night, kinda' drizzlin', and some clouds hummin' from the thunder, which is strange cause' to me, it hardly ever rains in the Bronx. Lil' D's knocked out while we're on our way back to the office. He only changed one trash can and knocked out like he don' cleaned to whole buildin'. Soft, just soft. Kinda' act like Cross when he got scared like a lil' ol' chicken. I feel sorry for the lil' ol' fella'. While I'm thinkin', the Geek just had the nerve to jump in his sleep, then jumped up chockin' from his snorin', then farted like he fired a Simi-Automatic gun. Nasty, just nasty. Kinda' funny. Me and Cross used to sit around and see who could fart the loudest. Man I miss ol' Cross, that was my boy and the good ol' days. "Are we there yet?" Lil' D' said while still tryin' to fart loud.

"Man you sound like that lil' boy on that movie when they were in the car traveling. We got about three more miles to go."

"That far? Wow I have to get home to watch my favorite television show Grays and the Anatomy."

"Is that what it's really called?"

"That's what I call it."

"Cool." I'm about to turn this Cat out. When I'm done with him he ain't gon' wanna' be no nerd again. "Say Lil' D' man, you wanna' roll with me tonight?"

"No Grays and the Anatomy's calling my name."

"How bout' some women callin' yo' name?" I smiled. I know he'd like that.

"Women? Uck! Women make me puke." He stuck his finger in his mouth. I laughed at how corney he is.

"Say Lil' D', have you ever been with a lady?"

"Women don't find me attractive. They think I'm from another planet," he said, putting his head down.

I'm sayin' to myself, you are. "Probably cause' of your style."

"I find my style very irresistible."

"Only in the eyes of the beholder."

"What?"

"I'm just playin'. Yo' man you gotta' come out of your shell, and only a female can change that."

"How can a female as you call her help me to come out of my shell?"

"Look lil' D' there's somethings that only a woman can give a man. And there's somethings that only a woman can say to a man to make him feel like a man—make em' feel real special. And there's somethings only a woman can do to make a boy become a man. And only a woman can bring out the best in a shelled up man. She knows how to touch us in the right places with her words and with her physical being (Genesis 2: 21-24). So you can't be crossing over to nothin' that claims to be a woman, but on his birth certificate it has a big brawny man's name on it" (Romans 1: 26- 32). We both laughed at the vision it gave. "See Lil' D, man women got that somethin', somethin', somethin' in the right place with the right moves, and right sex appeal that there ain't no searchin' after that. And with the right woman in yo' life, she can be all of those things to you; and with that she'll defiantly bring you out and you'll never go back in. So what's up, are you in tonight?"

"I'm in but I'll be very sad because Grays and the Anatomy calls my name on this night."

"Not tonight. Tonight's yo' night out on the town. Tonight's yo' night to come out."

"Should I be scared?"

"Awe' naw', just free." I laughed.

"I like being free, free to be myself."

"Just remember that when we get to where we're goin'. Did you tell me you ain't never been with no woman?"

"Thought I told you no?"

"Just wanted to make sure. So you're a virgin *(Romans 12:1)*?"

"If that's what you want to call it. Why, you want to spend the night with me?"

"Naw' Cat. I see you tryin' to have jokes huh'? A Gee don't roll like that. Women are this man's best friend."

"I thought dog's are a man's best friend?"

"You know what I'm sayin', you're a smart allick. Now if I tell Boss Man you ain't did nothin' when we get back how you gon' feel about that?"

"I'm just kidding. I know you're not a dog or a man lover. And I'm not either. I've just never had the guts to ask a nice girl out."

"I thought we were talkin' about that subject? Ha' yea' see you wanna' lil' fun, I knew it! You gon' be alright lil' man. But this is what I want you to do, I want you to call women, females, or gals, or ladies. Not girls."

"What's the difference?"

"Sayin' it like that makes you more relaxed. See Lil' D' man, you gotta' relax. You too up tight. Don't no female wanna' too up-tight, and too stiff Gee."

"Gee, who's Gee?"

"Gee is another word for a man that knows he got it goin' on."

"O' ok. Gee." We both laughed.

☃

Boss Man was waitin' at the front counter like somebody's daddy. He ran up to Lil' D' and slightly hit him on the shoulder. "So how did it go?"

Lil' D' looked at me then back at Boss Man. "O', it was an experience."

"Well good. I see you're going to fit right in. I knew you would." Boss Man looked at me as if to be proud. "Good job Joe, you did well."

I clocked out, walked out of the office with Lil' D' followin' me. "Yo' man you ready to do this?"

"I guess." He said, reluctantly.

"Cool, let's go. Trust me, you gon' be alright."

I jumped in my Benz with him followin' behind me in his lil' Volkswagon. I'm not gon' even change. I'm too ready to laugh at this nerd. Hope the lil' Gee find somebody to lay down with tonight.

Ch. 8

Stacy's Strip Club

The lights are dim and the spotlight's flashin' around the stage to set the mood. A haze of smoke is restin' in mid air, settin' the strip club atmosphere with the help of almost every man's table blowin' cancer sticks of cigarettes and cigars. Some got the nerve to throw up a toast to the ladies while they do their thang' at their own reserved table dance. The sounds of my boy Al is on the sound system, loud and clear in my ears which is a force to be reckoned with. Her moves are in slow motion. She got her back turned to me, my minds wonderin' how the rest of her looks. She slowly twirled down, and around, and up and down, wrapping around the long pole that's sittin' in the middle of the stage. Man, she's makin' me move down the pole with her. Every turn she's makin' is turnin' my roller coaster ride into a slow song. She finally turned and showed what she got. Her looks

99

are to kill. Men are all over her. Some puttin' money in and out of her top—the only thing that's left on. Everything else she threw into the crowd, men are throwin' their arms at her beggin' for their turn for attention. She's almost completely exposed. I'm just sittin' back checkin' out the scenery and what she got to offer, like I always do. I don't like to share. I like my own table attention. She looked over at me like she heard what I just thought. She slowly danced off the stage and is now slowly makin' her way a little closer towards me. I sipped on some vodka *(Romans 13:13)* and fired up a sweet cigar. I can't believe what I'm seein'. She looks familiar—I think I know this brawd—a famous model maybe? Man she got me sweatin'. Her body looks like a coke bottle. She got all the right curves in all the right places. Like I said befo', I'm a thug and a gangsta' in a teddy bear body. As hard as I look, I still got feelings. That's the part that makes me mad at the world, cause' the world judges too much *(Matthew 7:1)*. They think thugs and gangsta's don't have a soft side. I hurt too. I cry too. I love too. Just not where the world can see it, cause' it'll mess up my fly-ness. I laughed to myself. The image of her body came back in view, interrupted by the quick imagination. She turned her attention with her eyes over to my direction. We're makin' eye love. She's inviting me to join her while her finger is tellin' me to come see. She a trip. I smiled a little but not too much to give a way the fact that I'm diggin' her. I've been to a million-to-one strip clubs, but I ain't never seen no queen like this befo'. She dropped her top. Got my mind goin' in circles, round and round I'm goin'. Ha' that fool be trippin', it must be the weed *(Romans 12:1)*. Her long black curly hair, with smooth silky skin, and thick legs makes me wanna' touch. She must've heard my thoughts again cause' now she's slowly dancin' her way closer to my small round, one man table. I got somethin' waitin' on her, she betta' watch it. When she move, I move. When she breath, I breath. We both are movin' and dancin' in slow motion as she's gettin' closer to my space. I can't wait to watch her lead. Man I forgot all about Lil' D'. Must've ran and hid some where. He was sittin' with me, but now he's nowhere to be found. Wait a minute, I do know this chick. I can't believe this. I sat up in my lil' brown wooden chair. I wouldn't have ever thought she would've turn to this. She fooled a Gee, and I'm a pretty good judge of character. I can look at a woman and know what she's all about before she even open up her mouth. I wouldn't have ever known she looks like this. I never would've in a million years of this life thought she would've turned from this God she say she was supposed to be servin', to a call girl on center stage. When I first met this brawd, the way she came off I wouldn't have ever picked this side of her. Kinda' feel sorry for her. She just sat on my lap. I don't know why I didn't figure this out earlier. I guess it was the weed and the vodka cloudin' up my brain. Or maybe it was just the fact that I was caught up on how fine this female really is *(1 John 2:16)*. Man she got a beautiful body. An actress on the Hollywood scene huh'? Yea' right.

She's totally topless now. Evidently she don't know it's me. She got her eyes closed like she in another world—still movin' to the beat of ol' Al. I'm movin' too, tryin to keep up with her strip club freakiness. I slid my big hands around her thin waist as she made it move round and round. I pulled her closer to my chest as my mouth met hers. Her eyes popped open. She took one look at me straight in my eyes, jumped up, and ran to the back of the stage like she scared for her life. I know she shame. I ain't gon' even run after her. As high as I am, I feel sorry for her. It's a trip to cause' when I'm high, I normally don't feel nothin' for nobody. I ask myself, why she lie? Man that's crazy, thought she knew the Man Up-Stairs? Thought she was better than that? I know she wasn't expectin' me, especially with that lap dance. She must-a' got mad at the Man Up-Stairs like me. I'm trippin' on how she just ran out. As nasty and perverted as I am *(1 Thessalonians 4: 2-7)*, I feel bad about what I just saw. I'm thinkin' back to "the Reminisce". This lady wouldn't give it up no matter how hard I tried, but now, I've just seen all of her body and got a lap dance *(Romans 12:1)*.

I can't help but look across the large, dark, hazed-out club and notice Lil' D' being serenaded by three strippers. I laughed. One of em' is plattin' his hair, another one is twirlin' his nerdy glasses with one hand and beggin' for more money with the other one, while the third one is doin' her thang, that's not to mention. Its funny cause' I ain't never seen no nerd with his pants down to his ankles and his knees shakin'. Now I'm satisfied. I got what I brought him here for. I knew he'd get turned out. Too bad I didn't. The only thing I hate is what I seen with Candy. It's a trip too cause' don't no thug feel bad bout' lookin' at no woman, but it's somethin' about Candy that's makin' me feel the way that I do. Maybe its cause' she had contact with the Man Up-Stairs. I don't know *(Romans 8:1)*. Even though I don't live for Em', I still gotta' respect for Em'. Ever since I talked to the chick on the phone that's friends with Pricilla, I ain't never been the same. From my thoughts, to my dreams, on into my conscious. I can't say that they made me change but they sho' have made an emotional impact.

∽

I stayed outside until all of the strippers came out and left. Club time been over with. There's only one car left in the parking lot. I know it's hers. She gon' have to face me sooner or later.

She finally came outside. I started up the Benz and slowly drove over towards her candy apple convertible Mercedes.

I let down the window. "Say, yo' Candy!" I hollered from the Benz.

103

"Get away from me!" She yelled and kept walking fast towards the car. She kept dashing her head back at me and towards the direction of her car real fast.

"Can I talk to you?" I hollered.

"I don't wanna' talk to you!" She threw her bags in her trunk, slammed it down, and jumped in the car like I'm stalkin' her.

"Listen!" I jumped out of my car and rushed up to her. She started her car ready to take off. "Will you listen for just a minute? Can I get a minute of yo' time?"

"I told you Joe, I don't wanna' talk. Haven't you seen enough of me already? As far as I'm concerned we've already talked enough."

"I didn't say one word to you up in there."

"You didn't have to, your presence did!" She skidded off into the early, dark, morning atmosphere. I hurried up and jumped back into the Benz, cold from the cold early morning weather. The smoke comin' from my mouth is evidence.

All this commotion I forgot about Lil' D'. I looked at my cell to see if I got any calls only to notice that Lil' D' hit my cell an hour ago. I dialed the number back. "Yo' did somebody hit my number?"

"Of course, if I were dying I'd be a dead man by now," he said.

"Look Geek stop talkin' that nonsense, where you at?"

"I'm preoccupied if you know what I mean?" He burst out laughing.

The thought almost made me sick to my stomach. "Alright Chief, I see you hit it big. I'm proud of you. Tell me about it in a little while at the J.O.B. You know it's goin' on 2:45am?"

"Yes, very aware of the time. Sounds good about the rest." He hurried up and hung up the phone in my face with some females gigglin' in the background.

Somehow or another I know this ain't the life I wanna' live. Drinkin', drugin', women, sexin', stripin'—the same ol' thang. Get tired some time (John 8:36). Maybe I feel this way cause' of what I just seen. I can't shake this Candy chick. Thought she was close to the Man Up-Stairs. As thuggish as I am, with the Man Up-Stairs being the last thing on my mind, I had some type of respect for the Brawd until what I just seen. But she did look good though. I fired up a nice long Black & Mild Cross gave me from Paris before the Man Up-Stairs took em', took a long hard hit off of it, and drove my black self on to the crib.

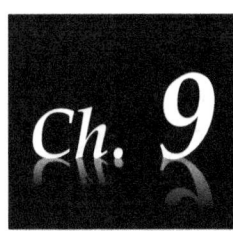

Ch. 9

I walked in the office to Boss Man's fussin'. It's an hour into clock time on the job and no sign of Lil' D'. Man I should've went and checked out who he was messin' with. I didn't think I needed to cause' he a grown man, and grown men usually can take care of themselves. Hope he didn't get robbed? One thing I forgot to tell em', these strippers don't play with their money.

ભ

Lil' D' finally walked through the door after bout' an hour, shakin'. I can't stop laughin'. "Yo' man Lil' D', you arite?"

Boss Man's lookin' at me crazy like I got somethin' to do with his disfuntionalism. "What's goin' on here?" He flashed his eyes at me like, I know you did this.

"As a matter of fact I'm feeling real good." Lil' D' answered. We both laughed but Boss Man didn't.

"That's my man." I reached to give em' dap. He looked at me crazy. "Yo man Lil' D' I'm tryin' to give you the thug's handshake."

"That's a thug's hand shake?"

"Yea' man, you'll get hip one day. Off of that..."

Boss Man burst in the conversation lookin' disgusted. "Yea', off of that and time to stop sittin' on my clock. Got some big orders for you two today." He pointed towards the front counter with all the orders sitting on the usual clip board. We all looked. He just looked at me disgusted. Lil' D' still shakin'. Seem like Boss Man got a little jealous—for what ever reason. Don't nobody get jealous unless they wanna' be close, or scared they gon' loose what they got, or ain't got no confidence to know who they are *(Song of Solomon 8:6)*.

I went and got the clip board from off the counter with Lil' D' followin' behind me. Boss Man got what he wanted and went in his office. We walked straight out to the junk ride, put the usual cleanin' stuff in the trunk, and took off to the first assignment.

"Say man, did you dig the club or what?"

"Yo' dude I dug," he tried to give me this off beat dap.

"Ok, now you goin' too far. Just stay a nerd. I mean, be yo' self," he laughed harder than me.

"Actually it was impeccable." I had to say, what? "Meaning it was faultless. It was perfect. All of the women were very nice and friendly."

"What kinda' friendly?"

"They were, well, they were friendly with everything."

"I bet they were. Man you crazy, ain't no stripper friendly. They all want one thang'—MONEY."

"No really, they were very nice. Yes money was a factor, but they were very nice and they made me feel very comfortable, so comfortable that it made me want to do anything and give them anything," he said, smiling like he thought about it.

"So did you?" I asked, firing up a cigarette.

"Yea' they turned my pockets inside out," he looked at me waitin' on me to laugh and I gave it to em'.

I laughed again almost chokin' on my cigarette. "Say man..." I coughed. "I got a lot to teach you. You make the chicks do all the work. You make them work for their coins."

"Actually I had dollar bills, not coins."

"There you go again, don't take it so personal, I'm just talkin' slang." I let him have it.

"Sorry."

"So how did they make a Chief feel?" I asked. I let down the window and flicked the cigarette out of the window.

"Felt good. I felt very important. I had all of their attention. I really liked the blond. She was hot. I'd like to go back. Hey can I ask you something?"

"Anything."

"Why were my pants so wet?"

"Maybe you wasted your drink on em'?" I laughed so hard I could barely drive. This Cat is the lord of the nerds, for real. I ain't never met nobody like this befo'. If my boy Cross was here, I know he would trip out.

"That's a good point," he said.

I laughed all the way to the first assignment which was the building I saw Ms. Candy at, leavin' Lil' D' wonderin' bout' that question he just asked about his wet pants.

α

Dirty and nasty as usual. One thing I'm glad about is Lil' D' followin' my lead. Ain't got to jack em' up, he's followin' my every command. Got em' down the hall changin' the trash, sweepin' the hallway, and vacuuming the front foyer. Me? Well I'm kickin' back for once. Takin' me a break. That lil' nerd owes me one anyway. Last time we were here, which was his first time on the J.O.B., he didn't do nothin' but threw up all day like a lil' ol' corporate american whimp. I wanna' take me a smoke break but Boss Man's time ain't nothin' to play with. A shadow of a Porto Rican woman came around the corner and caught my attention. I know I can tap that. I caught up with her. "How you doin', can I talk to you?"

"I'm sorry I'm working. Is it important?"

"It's important to tell you how beautiful I think you are." She laughed. I know I got her now.

"Well since you have this impressive since of humor, go ahead and talk. I have a few minutes." She set her brief case down on the carpeted floor.

"First of all I'm Joe, and yours?" I stuck out my hand waitin' on hers.

"Darlene." She met my hand and shook it soft and slow.

"You are so beautiful Darlene. Can't keep my eyes off of you. You're stunning."

"Why thank you." She said, blushing.

"I won't hold you long. I realize that you're hard at work and your time is valuable. I just had to stop you and give you that compliment and ask you for a dinner tonight?" She waited as if to think about it. "Please don't think too hard, you're breakin' a man's heart." I put my hand across my heart.

"You're rather charming.... I think I can do that." She took a pen and some paper out of her brief case and wrote her number down. "Here you go. Now I hope I'm not doing this for nothing?"

I took her hand and kissed it. "Not at all. Look forward to tonight. Anywhere special you like to eat?"

"I'll let your imagination do the talking, you seem to have a good one."

"Cool, I'll be by yo' crib, I mean, by your place before the sun goes down."

She laughed. "Charming. But don't you want to call first to find out where I live?"

"Just wanted to see if you were listening." I glanced down at the paper and back up at her beautiful short 5'3 height and size 5 shape. This' a shorty but she a fine shorty.

She started walking off down the hall, glanced back, smiled, and said, "look forward to it". She had the nerve to look sexy as she then turned shaking her long hair from side to side; as she kept walking down the hall towards her office.

I smiled back at her, "I won't let you down." I watched her curves move with every step she took.

This female made me sweat. It was hard talking politically correct. Don't know any thugs who talk politically correct. We talk slang. Ebonics is our buddy. I laughed to myself. I can't believe this brawd gave me her phone number and said yes to goin' out with me lookin' like that. I wonder what she got? Must got AIDS. She made it too easy to get the digits. Gotta' watch them kind. I likes me a challenge though. I was lookin' for her to look at me crazy and say that she don't go out with no janitors with dirty orange jump suits and black steel toe boots on. But she didn't. Maybe its cause' the trench dressed it up? Or maybe she was really diggin' my fly lines and handsome physique. Most of them tied lines I was doin' on purpose just to see where she was comin' from. Didn't take much which I don't like. The only way I'll call her is to see what she look like underneath that executive dress suit.

∞

The thought of Candy came back to my mind when I got to the same spot where we met up after ten years. I wonder if she still work here. Can't get over how she look. And the shame she went through when she found out it was me she was giving a lap dance to.

I walked down the hall to P & P Attorneys At Law and peaked in to see a Hispanic woman sittin' at her desk typing on the computer. "Excuse me mam', is Candy working today?"

She looked up. "No, I'm sorry, Candy no longer works here." She went back to typing.

"If you don't mind, can you tell me when she quit?"

"She called in and just told us that she quit about an hour ago."

"Do you know the reason?"

"I'm sorry I can't give that information. You would have to be her husband or a relative. Are you her husband?" She asked.

I'm thinkin' to myself I wish. "No, just a concerned friend."

"O' that's nice, but she's no longer here. Maybe you can call her?"

"Yea' maybe so, thanks." I closed the office door broken hearted. I'm thinkin' about what she just said. Don't that brawd think if I had Candy's phone number I wouldn't have went in there lookin' for her? Crazy, I thought to myself. Some people don't think about what they gon' say before they say it.

Can't look her number up in the phone book cause' I know it's not listed. Maybe I can go back to the strip club tonight and hope that she'll be up there. I know Lil' D'll be ready to go.

୪

"Yo' Lil' D'!" I yelled from the lil' G-ride that's strickly for business. He came runnin' out of the glass door pullin' up his pants from his ankles. "Man, yo' what up, what's yo' problem?"

"Had to take a leak." He rushed and got in as I quickly backed out of the parkin' lot and sped down the road laughin' cause' he forgot to zip his fly.

"I see you startin' to talk like a Gee. I like your effort. Keep tryin'."

"I'm just tryin' to be down dude." He cheesed at me with his milky yellow teeth that look like they haven't been brushed in months; and had the nerve to have a bright yellow shine to em'.

"Ok, leave the word dude out and you got it." I laughed.

"Cool."

I burst out laughing again. "Now you tryin' too hard. Just chill and be yourself."

"Every time I'm myself people laugh at me. They say mean things like: 'You got Ercle beat', or 'you look like a phony Ercle'. I hate that."

"Yo' man, you just gotta' blast em' and be done with it."

114

"Look Joe, I'm not into shooting people. I'm not a killer."
He started pouting with his mouth.

"Killa'? Who said anything about bein' a killa'? I'm talkin'
bout' goin' off on em'."

"No." He shook his head real fast. "I'm not going to spray
some Off Repelente on them either. I'm not a gangsta' like you
Joe."

"Strike three. You still lost. I was talking about tellin' em'
off. You know? Like givin' them a peace of your mind?"

He shook his head real fast again. "No, and I'm not going to
tell them what's on my mind. Because when you tell what's on
your mind, people may not like what you have to say. I'll just
keep quiet like I've been doing."

"Done, cause' you stupid man. You can't even see what I'm
talkin' bout'. I'm on yo' side." Things got quiet.

I guess Lil' D got hot at me. He didn't say anything all the
way back to the office to return the car and end the day.

怆

As soon as I put the clipboard down on the counter, Boss Man
couldn't wait to see if we made all the rounds. He ran over
and thumbed through the files on the clip board like it was
cash. Me and Lil' D' just stood there lookin', waitin' on him to
say somethin' negative. To our surprise, he didn't say nothin',
just shook his head as if to agree. I turned and looked at Lil' D
and nearly burst out laughin' again to the fact that he still

haven't zipped his fly up. I know Blondie is gettin' a good look cause' she can't keep her eyes off of him.

Boss Man walked back in his office without sayin' a word, I guess that means we free to go. I can't wait cause' I got a fine woman and a hot dinner waitin' on me tonight.

I gave Blondie one look. "I see you like what you see?" I looked at Lil' D and back at her and smiled.

"Mind your own business. I look at what I want."

"You right. I could care less. Just don't try nothin' with my boy. He's not cho' type." I walked up and leaned over the counter and got in her face.

"You better back off before I have your job." She said, backing back.

"Don't nobody want chu', you too mean. You might could get a date if you wasn't so mean and grouchy."

"And you might could get a better job if you would learn how to talk, Mr. Ebonics." She laughed.

To my surprise Lil' D burst in with his two cents. "I'll take her out." His glasses are still thicker than a coke bottle. "You want to go out with me tonight?" He brushed pass me as she came from around the counter and met his offer with a quick surprised, "yes". She nodded her head like she sizzlin' hot. Probably ain't had none in I don't know when.

He took her arm and wrapped it around his and took her to the back to get her things, and they were out like a twisted couple for the world to laugh at.

As they walked out, their voices faded into the air. I could hear Lil' D say, "is Micky D's good enough?" I tripped out.

ᚪ

I couldn't wait to blow Darlene's cell up. I'm ready to see what she's all about. Top Corporate American woman and thangs. I like them kind, feisty, and ready.

I ain't never met nobody so real in my life except Pricilla. Darlene surprised me. Lookin' at her in that building I would have never thought she was a private Investigator let alone a minister. Yea' I said a minister. After I took her out she had the nerve to check me before I even asked her to go to the crib with me; and let me make her feel like a special lady. I guess the Man Upstairs who I totally disagree with, must've told her. Same mess Pricilla used to come at me with. I wonder how can one Man, or Thing, or Invisible Being talk to two different people that ain't never met each other at the same time? Who live in two totally different places and two totally different parts of the city at the same time? He kinda' got my attention somewhat, but I'm still determined not to give in and let Him have His way. Now I know why she was so quick to give me those digits. It was a set-up to get me alone with her so she could trap me with those Jesus words. She still fine though. I let her loose. Almost let her out of my Benz right after we left the restaurant. That's how frustrated I was when she said she wasn't gon' give it up. Talkin' bout' the only Man she'll give it up to is Jesus. That made me so mad I almost hit her. That made me mad cause' I couldn't get my way. I always get my way with women. It ain't too many of em' that deny my charm. Maybe my time has come to make a change. I'm too stubborn to change. She mentioned she's a Private Investigator who helps people find their lost family members; I wonder who she be tryin' to find? I laid across my sofa pissed off like a bum who just drunk his last bottle of booze.

My cell blew up just as that thought came across my mind. Some unfamiliar digits. "Who dis?" I answered with my stern, ain't got no time for no junk cause' I can't get none, voice.

"How are you?" She asked. Her voice is unfamiliar at the moment, but very soft and believing.

"Who you wanna' talk to?" I asked.

"This is Joe's phone number?"

"Yea' dis' Joe. Who dis'?"

"This is Darlene. Please don't hang up. I know we departed on not so good terms, but I wanted to call you because something's heavy on my mind. I can't get the thought off of my mind about what you said on yesterday."

"What did I say? O' bout' you givin' it up and you tellin' me no?" I raised up then fell back down on the sofa.

"Not nearly. I'm talking about, well, I guess you don't remember you telling me about you not knowing who, and where your brothers and sisters are over dinner at the restaurant. As you know I am a Private Investigator who find families who have been broken a part. I told you that in so many words on yesterday. I thought about it all night as to why you were sent in my path. I always ask God that question when or after I meet a person. Of course the thought of your constant request of making me feel special came as well." She softly chuckled to herself. "But the fact that I'm sold out to God, I couldn't make your request come true. I want you to know that I'm only calling because there's an assignment I have with you. God has assigned me to help you look for your brothers and sisters. I believe this was a prayer of yours."

"What? How did you know that?" I asked, almost fallin' off the long sofa.

"The Lord revealed it to me on last night." She answered with the quickness.

"Revealed? Man ya'll some witches. Ya'll got some physic powers from the devil. I don't want no part of that crazy sicko', psychic maniac stuff. I tell you what you ain't got to help me cause you lyin'. God ain't told you that. I told you about me bein' divided from my brothers and sisters. So this business about God revealin' my business to you is a joke lie!"

"Why are you so cold harded? God has tried to prove Himself to you so many times. He has given you so many chances to come to Him and totally surrender your life to Him. And the thing about it is the fact that you do not believe in Him. You hate Him, treat Him evil, and are constantly bucking against His people who He has sent in your path to help you. One minute you believe, the next minute you don't. Although you're confused, He still loves you and is still trying to help you. God is merciful and kind *(1 Chronicles 16:34)*. No matter how evil and confused people are to Him, He still loves them and He'll do whatever it takes to draw them to Him. And He's drawing you now. God has a work for you to do Joe and this is my assignment to help you, only if you want it because God gives you a choice *(Matthew 22:14)*. He does not pressure you or make bad things happened to you. You do that on your own *(Joshua 24:15)*."

"Man that's the same thing my ex used to say to me befo' she left me alone. Why is God so worried about me?"

"Because He cares about your soul and He has a work for you to do. He doesn't want you to go to Hell."

"What's up with Hell? What is it and where is it?"

"Hell is a place of eternal damnation *(Psalms 9:17)*. If you go there you'll never come back. You'll never have a chance to give your life to God. You'll burn there eternally. There's no coming back, that's why He's beckoning you to choose Him today and surrender your life to Him. You have an Atheist spirit—a spirit that does not believe in God *(Mark 16:14, Acts 19:9)*. He wants you to know that He is real. He is not some evil thing that comes to confuse you and mess your mind up, thinking something that's not real. He's given you all the clues to know that He is real and that He's not trying to hurt you, He's trying to help you."

Once again I can't say nothin'. This brawd has put a dent on my brain and a hidden fear in my heart. Candy got this same way with words. Even Pricilla's homegirl from church, I think her name was Sabrina. What's up with all these Christian women? They all sorta' alike. "I don't know what I'm gon' do. I do wanna' find my brothers and sisters. If you gon' help me, then help me. But don't start somethin' you can't finish."

"After I obey the Lord is when I'll be finish. I'm not here to please man, I'm here to please the Lord."

ℜ

I stayed quiet as me and Darlene finished our conversation— which was about another hour and a half. Her set up on findin' my brothers and sisters came real smooth. I'm waitin' to see what she got.

ℜ

My bed feels real good after a long day's work and a night's happy hour. Feels like a man's kingdom and a relaxation crib castle. I flipped the channels on the 72 inch screen like I can't run out of stations. Every female I see on each channel looks like that chick Candy. She got my mind turnin' circles. I ask myself why she lied to me bout' bein' an actress? Why didn't she just tell me the truth? I think I'm gon' try and find her somewhere, anywhere. I gotta' find that brawd.

Darlene gotta' Gee's thoughts too. Can't get the psychic message she said off my mind. I wonder if the Man Upstairs really communicated with her? That's a question I'll forever ask myself. Too many fony religious freaks out there. If she was so close to Em', why she led me on and made me think she was gon' give it up? Crazy. It'll take more than that to make me believe.

ଔ

The trench comes right in handy in this late December. The Bronx is very cold and busy. As sorry as Kizzy's Janitorial Service is, it got the nerve to be in the same area as the high, big time Towers in the middle of New York's Downtown. The old woodened two office, one bathroom for the guys and ladies to share; and the waitin' area in the front as crazy customers walk in, discourages anybody from gettin' any service there. I guess the tower's is what draws em'. I quit tryin' to take the Benz to work. Now I'm smart. I take the subway. I caught the first one that would let me. Crowded as usual. Hobo's, pimps, prostitutes, small and big time business men and women runnin' all over the place; and talkin' their own talk.

The subway is on time. Good. The doors flew open and the rush of over a thousand people rushed to get through the double sliding doors. If I was still on the streets, I would shoot every last one of em'. Instead I'm just gon' go with the flow.

ଔ

When the midget office building came in view, I found it the same as usual accept Boss Man standin' outside lookin' like he got a lot on his mind. Standin' outside is unsual for him but somethin' ain't right. He took out a cigarette, fired it up, and puffed on it a hundred miles per hour. "Yo' what up Boss Man? Why you standin' out here?" I asked, tryin' to go through the motions of life and cold-hearted reality.

He flicked the almost done cigarette on the sidewalk. "Life man. Life. I don't think you gon' have your job much longer. I'm filing for bankruptcy. I can't do this no more."

He tried walking off but my words wouldn't let em'. "Yo' man what' chu' tryin' to say? I'm fired just like that? This job is all I got!"

"Awe' man, you a strong Cat, you'll find a new one quick."

I could pop him in his mouth and blow his head off with a 45- Automatic. "Yo' man maybe you didn't hear me. I said this job is all I got!" I walked up to him.

He threw his hands up to brace himself. "I heard you and did you hear me? I can't do this no more! You're not a business owner, you don't understand! Things happen Joe! Jobs come and go! You'll be alright." He yelled, as the cold morning smoke blew from his mouth.

"Where's everybody else? Where's David? Have you fired him too? Where's Blonde, I mean yo' receptionist? So you just gon' get rid of all of us? Man that's a low blow! That's low down and dirty man! You could've handled it better than this way. Where I'm gon' go? Who gon' help me Man?"

He brushed me off with his hand. "I'm through. Get your things and I'll give you your last check. Now you're really free to go. I know you've been waiting on this moment anyway. All you do is talk down on my company. You don't care nothing about this company no way Joe!"

"Yo' man you right but it's still my job! And I need my job!" I wanna' shoot his head off but I can't go back to the pen. A blow to the face was the next thing he felt. I hit em' so hard he flew back and fell up against his car. He shook his head in disbelief as the blood from the wound from his eye streamed down the side of his face. He rushed me and grabbed me around my waist like a weak ol' man and tried to tackle me on the small graveled parking lot. His strength wasn't strong enough to throw me down on the ground instead it wrinkled my trench and that pissed me off all over again. I upper cutted em' in the face, but he had it covered with both of his hands like a lil' gal. I gave up feelin' sorry for the ol' Cat, and for what I just did. I lost it. All I can think about is how I gave up the game to this sorry no payin' job, then to get fired when I could have had it all. His attitude is what got em' a black eye. Hadn't been runnin' his mouth, he wouldn't of got popped. I ain't did that in years. I tried walkin' off down the street but couldn't cause his loud cries stopped me. The bro' is really havin' it bad. For some reason I feel sorry for em'. I walked back and helped him get up off the gravel. Surprisingly he let me. Probably didn't wanna' get popped again. "Say man, get up. All you had to do is let me keep my job."

"I can't see. I can't see." He tried wiping the blood from his eye and tried to get up off the gravel at the same time.

"Calm down. All you gotta' do is relax and look." I tried not to laugh. I shouldn't have hit em'. He an ol' man. Ol' men can't fight back. "I didn't wanna' hit you but I couldn't take you talkin' crazy to me no mo'."

"Awe' man you like all the rest of those Cats. All ya'll wanna' do is fight when ya'll can't get ya'll way. This is why I'm givin' this mess up."

"Say man all you gotta' do is get you a loan." I said, sitting him on the curb.

"Loans are hard to come by, especially with a black man being the CEO. The banks ain't tryin' to help a brother like myself." He took a hankie from his coat and wiped his face again.

"Have you tried?" I stepped up to em'. Kinda' felt like a close relative just that quick.

"Naw'. I already know what they're going to say. I got a loan years ago and had to go through a bunch of bull just to get it! And then it wasn't what I asked for. It was way under half of what I asked for and that's why I ended up in this ol' shack of a building and not in one of those towers you see all around us."

I can't say nothin'. I ain't never owned no business but I was my own boss runnin' the streets and the women. I don't know how it feel when thangs don't go my way, cause' I've always had everything go my way; even the women. The police even obeyed my command. "Say man I hear you. Can't say I understand, but I hear you."

He stood up and walked towards the building and turned around and said, "I'm too old for this man. I don't know what I'm gon' do. I'll keep your position in mind if I decide to keep on going, but as of today I don't think so." He said, slowly staggered his way into the building and disappearing behind the glass door. I feel like that's the last time I'm gon' see Mr. Kizzy, I mean Boss Man again as I left walkin' back towards the Subway.

⌇

My cell went on blast as the digits of "the Nerd David" flashed on the screen. "Yo' dis' Joe."

"Joe, hi this is David, the guy you work with at Kizzy's Janitorial Service."

"No kidding cherlock. I know who you are idiot. When you gon' stop being a nerd?"

"When you respect me as one." He chuckled as if his comeback was a good one.

"Still stupid. What do you want? I assume you wanna' know where yo' job is?"

"That is correct. Where is it? Our boss will not talk to me. All he said is 'don't come back anymore. Very unprofessional don't you agree?"

"I agree that I'm pissed that I don't have a job no more! Say what you gotta' say!"

"Why are you yelling at me I didn't fire you?"

"Cause' you stupid and gettin' on my nerves you idiot."

"I thought you were my friend?" He started crying like Kizzy did after I popped em' in the eye.

"Say man don't start winnin' like a lil' girl. I'm still yo' friend I'm just mad at the fact that I have no job and nowhere to go."

"I hear ya' kido. It doesn't feel very good."

I got quiet and he did too. After a moment of silence, I pressed the button that says "end". We both parted our ways and I don't know when I'll ever see or talk to the nerd again.

Meetin' Darlene for our first real meeting without me tryin' to get with her is a hard thing to look forward to. I can say she's keepin' her promise. She ain't let up these past few weeks. She had a couple of leads but none turned out successful yet. The way this brawd's goin' I know she gon' find em' real soon.

My phone lit up 'Darlene'. I picked up on the first ring with her words, "Hey this' Darlene. Are you ready for our journey? I have some leads."

"Ready when you are beautiful."

"Please don't come with the charm. This is business and not pleasure."

"It was worth a try. Say, why you so strong?" I had to ask.

"I have to be."

"Why? I didn't ask you to bed?"

"That doesn't matter. I don't want you to get comfortable. We're on a mission to find someone dear to you and my assignment is way too important than trying to tantalize your flesh."

"Ok, ok enough of the bible words. I give up. Business is what it is." I almost threw the phone down. "Where to first boss?"

"I figure you can come down to the station and I'll show you some leads from my computer and we can go from there. Sounds good?"

"Cool. I'm on my way."

"How're you going to get here, I never gave you the address?"

"O' yea' that's right. You gotta' Gee on his knees. Where's the place Ms. Lady?" I asked, smiling at her cunning words.

"It's on Allen Street…"

I cut her off. "I know where that building is."

"But you didn't let me finish." She said, got the nerve to get a slight impatient attitude.

"I didn't have to. I'm the King of the Bronx. I know where every street is."

"O' ok. See you when you get here. I'm in suite 443. I guess you know where that is to, huh'?" I can tell she smiled without makin' a sound.

"Yep. Got it. On my way." I looked a little crazy with a smirk that went into a slight smile.

ભ

Just like she said I didn't let her finish. Hate I didn't. Got lost and had to call her four times like a whimp cause'. The old life has been a while, and the thought of where all the roads is, is a little foggy. The big white building stood out among all the rest as it stood in my fore view. I walked up the concrete stairs as if I was walking up the stairs to the White House, just not that many. As soon as I got to her office door, sweat started pouring down the side of my face. I'm nervous from the unexpected. Never seen my siblings before and don't know if they'll receive me or not. It ain't but a hand full of em'. Don't know how long it's gon' take to find em'. Don't know why I was chosen to find em' anyway. Why would the Man Upstairs pick me and send a gorgeous lady to help me? I'm pondering over it all and maybe, just maybe it's startin' to make an impact on a Gee. I fired up a hand made cigarette, took two puffs, and put it out on the wall with my hand with the thoughts Mom's. One of my boys called me and told me Mom's over-dosed in some crack house. I set her up a quick funeral and waited for them to quickly put her in the ground. I know I sound coal, but I'm still mad cause she wasn't much of a positive supportive mom's in my life like she should've been. Half the time I never knew where she was. O' well, maybe she in peace now?...

ભ

The doors flew open without me opening em'. A room full of young and old people stood looking at me as if to be nervous and surprised. Darlene is the first to grab me and hug me. "Surprise! Come on in. Here are all of your siblings! They have all been found. I found them on last week but didn't want to tell you. I wanted it to be a surprise. Are you surprised?"

"I'm without words. I never thought you had already did this for me? All ya'll my pep's?"

They all started crying and some laughed with happiness. We all cried for a while. Even a Gee cried for about an hour. I often wonder why my Pops had so many kids. Kinda' feel like they still all not here.

CB

My bed is full of roaming thoughts. Most of my sisters and brothers live in foster homes and, or married with kids. They seem too happy to reunite with me. Not much was said except why Pops didn't love us and bring us together. We all supposed to get together and hang out soon considering it's been two weeks already. My cell blew up with Darlene's name highlighted on the screen. "Yea' dis' Joe?" I answered on the first ring.

"Hey Joe there's something I need to tell you. I know you're overwhelmed about finding your siblings but there's just one more thing I need to tell you. I did not find all of your siblings like I thought I did. There's still one more person, your sister. Her name is Brenda. She's in a crack house in San Antonio,

Texas. Your middle brother called me back and told me after everyone had left. He didn't want to cause any friction. He doesn't know how to reach her. She doesn't want any help. She just want to be left alone. He's the only sibling she thinks she has. She don't know about the other siblings. She doesn't even know your dad—just heard of em' from your brother. You guys are in the same boat. She's been in and out of jail and the pen. Beat up and left for dead numerous of times. She's also lived here at one time, but left with some dude and is now stuck up there in Texas. Your brother gave me the address where he believes she's located. He thinks it's a crack house she's staying in, but there's no police record of it. Do you want to fly down to meet her? Maybe we can talk her into coming back?"

"Man that's a dagger in my heart. I hate to hear that. I don't know what to do. I guess. What I'm gon' do?" I put my head down in thought and in shame. All I can think about is the thousands I poisoned who bought crack and weed from me. Now I'm hearin' that my own sista' is a victim. I used to laugh at crack heads and dope heads as they struggled to find money to buy from me. They begged and begged and would give up their life just to get a piece of rock. I would laugh and hit em' just for the fun of it. Now it's my own sista' that needs my help. "D, I don't think I can do it."

"What? Why not? This is what you and I've been waiting for. This is a chance in a life time. Most don't find their siblings but you almost have. What's the problem?" She asked.

"I'm dealin' with my past life. I was the one who fed crack heads the crack. I was the one who poisoned em' as they begged for my goods. I was the one who killed and left many for dead without ever bein' caught. I was the one who didn't care whether people lived or died. All I wanted was the cash, the women, the drug-lord life style, and all the power. I'm an ex- dope dealer. But that don't make me a thug. I'm a thug, not because of my life style, but because of who I am. Not because I sold drugs and was a drug lord, but because of my style and my flavor."

She waited for a second before addin' in her words. This' somethin' Darlene's good with. She know how to listen. "Joe, everybody has a past. I'm glad that's your past and not your present life. I'm sure your sister, being in the condition she's in will not ask you what did you used to do. I believe the only thing that will be on her mind is PLEASE HELP ME. People in that position may not seem as if they want help, but they do. They just don't know how to reach out because people are always judging them. All they need is for people not to judge them, love them, and help them."

"I feel ya'. It's cool, you've convinced me. We can do that. I'll meet you at your office in the morning. We can take the first plane out."

"That's fine. I look forward to it." She said as if to be about to hang up the phone.

"Darlene wait! Don't hang up the phone!"

"I'm still here. What's going on?"

"I just wanna' say thank you for all yo' help in this. You a strong female, I mean woman and I admire that."

"Why thank you Joe. You're a very strong man and God is doing a mighty work in you even as I speak, and you don't even know it."

"Ok I'm off the phone with that. Not quite ready for those words but it's cool. I'll see you tomorrow Pastor D." We both laughed and hung up the phone at the same time.

ೞ

The plane ride is a bumpy one. Turbulence is the pilot of the plane. My sleep is disturbed. Darlene haven't stopped readin' some thick book ever since we stepped foot on this plane. I'm kinda' jealous. I like all the attention and I'm not gettin' it to some book. This chick is somethin' special. I can't see myself with her, but maybe if Cross was still here I could maybe fix him up with her. He was much more sensitive. Ms. D' seem like she a little sensitive. I would hurt her and that is not an option in my world. I could get along with her body but her sensitivity might be too overwhelming.

As the plane bumped a long, I got some time to think about my future with the workin' world. Do I go back to the game or do I look for another job? These are questions that need an answer and quick. A brother got bills and needs. Don't no woman want no broke man.

CB

The plane released us to slight on and off rain in San Antonio, Texas. We took the first taxi available. Darlene guided the taxi driver straight to the crack house's address. I can barely look at the barely standin' shack where the sister I never met is wastin' her life away in. The question of will she believe that I'm her brother ran cross my mind? Most crack heads are in a totally different world when they on that stuff. She probably won't even know I'm a man. I don't think this was a good idea.

"Having second thoughts?" Darlene asked, taking a quick glance at me and back out of the taxi window as if she read my thoughts. She tapped the back of the taxi driver's seat. "Right here driver, this' our stop." The taxi slowed down to a complete stop right in front of what looks like a boarded run-down shack. Paint is chafed off on every board, and some of the boards are sayin' find me. Impossible to have any life up in there. Most crack houses have crack heads runnin' in and out. At least some kind've life. Strange. Just strange.

We're just sittin' here looking and thinking. I finally spoke up after a moment of silence. "How did you know?"

She smiled, swung her head back, and looked me straight in my eyes and answered, "By your facial expression."

"I hate it's tellin' it all. This woman won't be in her right mind. Plus she ain't never met me befo' and probably won't think I'm her brother. Maybe you should go up in there and bring her out and..." I gave her a dead stare.

"Tell you what. For your peace and safety and mine, I'll wait and get the police to get her out and we'll go from there. I got some friends that will help."

"Cool."

After we got out, Darlene reached through the window and paid the cab driver. He sped off like he was scared to wait for us to change our minds.

Just when we walked up to the raggedy door, Darlene dialed the fuzz' digits on her cell for help. I forgot just that quick bout' her bein' a detective and all.

She got one police car over with the quickness. Man, she got some connections. She spoke up as they slowly stepped out the car. "Hi Tom, hi John."

"Hi Darlene, it's been awhile since you've been on our turf." The two Caucasians looked at each other and chuckled. Their appearance fits two professional boxers that ain't never lost a match. Bout' 6 feet each and 250 lbs. One red head and the other with coal black hair with none at the top.

Darlene laughed like what they said was so funny—I don't think so. "I know, I know it's been awhile but glad you guys could get right over here. We have a situation that I need you guys to handle. You know you owe me one right?" She smiled like they had secrets between em'. I'm hopin' they don't see my past, cause' I got a big one with em'.

"Sure anything for you." I guess that's Tom she talkin' to cause' she ain't even introduced me yet.

She can't stop laughin', startin' to get on my nerves a little. "O' Tom, you're something else." She turned and looked at me like she heard my thoughts again. Kinda' scary. "Hey Tom and John this' why we're here. This' Joe Quick, the guy I was telling you guy's about. As you know his sister is inside of there and we just want to get her out as quick and as peaceful as possible. I know there's no search warrants involved but I guess we can just try to see if she will come out anyway."

They walked up to me as if they're about to take me in, but reached for my hand shake and I gave it to em' real fast. "Nice to meet you Joe. Hopefully we can make your day and give you what you came for. This' an old run down house that hasn't been kept up nor has seen family life in decades." John waved his hands in the air and looked out into the San Antonio atmosphere. "And as you can see this' a neighborhood that hasn't seen a wholesome, peaceful family life in decades. Wow what's wrong with our world?"

"I hear ya' man but I'm determined to get my sista' and take her home to the rest of my sista's and brotha's."

"Sure, we understand. No sign of life in there, hopefully she's in there." Tom turned and looked at Darlene for further instructions.

She spoke up real quick. "This is the only address I have... Ok, well, here we go. Hey guys, Joe and I aren't ganna' go in, we'll wait for you guys to come out. Hopefully you'll come out with her." She gave me this worried but hopeful look. They barely took two steps and Darlene changed her mind. "Hey I don't think you guys should go in. For some reason I feel it's not going to work. I don't think it's a good thing to do."

Tom was the first to speak up. "Fine, just call us if you have problems." He looked at John. "We won't be far." They went and got in the car and left speedin' down the street like they just got a tip on a missin' fugitive.

⋈

Night is fallen fast. The coolness of the late evening makes me glad I got my trench to keep me warm. Darlene went and came back after gettin' us a couple of candy bars and some chips while I sat on the curb for about an hour. Why it took her so long I don't know. I dare not ask cause' she kinda' grouchy. Kinda' look like she's givin' up a little as she joined me on the curb. Earlier we knocked on the door for thirty whole minutes. I tried walkin' around the back but didn't get far cause trash, high grass, and old dirty furniture cluttered my path. No sign of life from this shack yet as we're now in the front yard sittin' on the curb. I know Darlene's giving up. She hasn't told me with her mouth, but with her eyes. I'm bout' to give up too.

Just as my thoughts are about to become a reality, to our surprise a dirty lookin' woman who looks like she been sleep for days came out the house; and sat out on the porch like she didn't even see us, or know that we been out here for over an hour. For some reason she looked like she crossed my path befo' or had some dealings with her. Me and Darlene didn't hesitate to get up from the curb and slowly go approach her. Darlene spoke up first. "Hey what's your name?" The lady looked up at her and gave her this I'll knock you out look as she weakly raised both of her fist.

"Brenda. Why? You the po po?" Darlene cracked a huge smile and gave me this we got our lady but be quiet and don't spoil the surprise yet look. I barely obeyed.

"No, I just wanna' know your name. Look we didn't come here to harm you nor take you in, so don't worry."

"I ain't got nothin' for you no way." She got up off the porch and tried to walk back in the house but thought about it and waited by the door, lookin' back at us.

Her presence is somethin' no woman should ever want to look like. Her smell is horrendous. She look like her life should end right now. A hundred pounds and anorexia is her name. I hate somebody popped her, she ain't got but two teeth in the front with a day ol' black eye. Man I hate this. For once I feel sorry. I ain't never felt sorry for no crack head, let alone no female. I just hate it's my sista', so I think. Something is changing in me and I don't like it. I can't get soft like a female.

I'm a hard Gee and a thug at heart and can't nobody change that—not even the Man Upstairs.

Brenda looked out at me from the porch. "Hey. Don't I know you?" She came charging towards me.

Backin' up was my first thoughts. "Naw' you ain't got no dealings with me."

"Yes I do, you the one who got me hooked on this stuff!" She pointed her finger in my face. "I may be blowed out and look crazy but I do have sense and I know you're the one who got me hooked on this stuff! You're that guy who is very known in the Bronx. I used to live there. You sold drugs to a lot of people. You had that good stuff that I couldn't get enough of. I never would've let you get me hooked had I not needed the money to feed my eight children. I needed some quick cash and you were available. Don't you remember our night together?"

I tried backing up some more. Shame, embarrassment, and a sick feeling just came over me all at the same time. "Look I'm not the one. You blowed out and seeing thangs."

"No I'm not. I'm a very smart lady with a photographic memory. I may be sick on this stuff but I can remember anything whether I'm high or not. I do know what I'm talkin' bout'. Answer this question. Did you sell drugs?"

"Yea' so what?"

"Did you sell to a lot of people?"

"Yea."

"Were you well known?"

"Look you gettin' way too personal." I said.

Darlene's lookin' at me like just tell her the truth but instead she jumped in. "Look Brenda. We came all the way down here for a reason. And the reason is you. What if I tell you that this is your brother? Would you believe me?" She asked. She looked confused, looking at Darlene and then at me.

"I don't know cause' we slept together. If he is, that's messed up that I slept with my brother for drugs and I didn't even know. I don't know what he has now, but he had a good way with words plus I was high and wanted to get higher. He had the goods and the sex appeal. I was turned on immediately by his smooth words and his sexy touch. I wanted him to give me some of that good stuff he used to give me." She burst out laughin' in a sick, high hysterical way.

"Look Brenda I'm sorry that I did that to you. If I would've known you were my sista' I wouldn't have came at you like that. I would've tried to help you. That's sick even thinkin' bout' it. My whole situation and past is all messed. I feel bad about the thousands of lives I messed up. Some still here. Some gone. I gotta' lot of blood on my hands and I didn't mean to mess yo' life up." She burst out cryin', and I can pass out right bout' now.

"This' some messed up s@%t!" She threw herself on the grass and cried harder.

Some Taho just drove up. Some dude bout' 6'7 just jumped out and ran and grabbed Brenda from off the grass. "B@%&h, get up! I tol' you not to be talkin' to nobody!" He punched her in the face. The force of his fist threw her in a complete circle and back down on the grass just that quick. Me and Darlene didn't have time to react. "Get up! I said get up!" He picked her up but stopped when I jumped in, grabbed him and punched him in the mouth; and threw him down on the grassy but still paved driveway. That was his last time layin' a hand on my sista'. He picked himself up off the ground, spit a couple of bloody teeth out and grabbed his mouth tryin' to stop the blood from hittin' the ground. He stumbled back into his Taho and drove off cursing like he got the best of me.

"If you ever lay a hand on my sista' again, I'll kill you!" I yelled into the air. I tried followin' the truck down the street as I crossed over the high, grassy front yard but Darlene stopped me from goin' further.

"Brenda look it's time for you to move! Aren't you tired of gettin' beat?" Darlene yelled from across the yard.

"Been tired." Her cries mixed her words and moans.

"So are you coming with us? We're taking you back to the Bronx." Darlene spoke up with authority as we both walked up to her.

"I don't think I can go. He'll kill me."

I had to jump in. I grabbed her shoulders. "Look lil' Sis'. I'm here to take you home. That idiot ain't gon' do nothin' to you."

145

"You don't understand. You've always been the one who used to beat women so I know you don't understand. I used to watch you from a distance out on the corner."

I'm speechless. I ask myself, why is it different? Is it different cause' this' my sista' and not some other female? Man, I hate this position. I let her shoulders go and stepped back.

Darlene saved the day. "Joe help me get her up. We're taking her back right after we take her to a close by gas station and clean her up. I got some extra clothes in my bag."

挈

This plane is much smoother than the other one. Got my sista' right by my side without a fight. Darlene got a good way with words. They worked. Brenda didn't even pack. Her body is her luggage. My only thought is, where's the eight kids? Maybe that'll come later.

Ch. 12

Darlene put **Brenda in a Halfway** house and a got her some therapy for her drug addiction. Hope its workin'. As for me, I'm tryin' to avoid Darlene cause' right now I need me some. I ain't tryin' to become no Saint. I need a woman and I need one right now. Let me see who I can call first. I scrolled through my contacts to come to my ol' flame Pricilla. Should I call her? How would she take to me, it's been a couple of years? The phone blew up in my hands. "Dis' Joe."

"What up Boss?" An unfamiliar voice said, tryin' to make me know who he is. "Who dis'?" I shot back.

"Dis' Chew Baby."

I can't believe it. This is one of the young fella's who went out to rob with me and Cross. "What up man? Whata' surprise."

"Yea' I found yo' number on my ol' cell I thought I threw it away. Hey man you still runnin' the game and doin' yo thang?"

"Naw' man I ain't done that in years. What up? You doin' it now?"

"Yea' I never stopped and I need yo' help. I know you been missin' in action but I got some big cash if you want it?" He said, hopin' I'll agree.

"How much cash you talkin' and what chu' got for me?"

"30 g's. All you gotta' do is drive and watch while we go in and do our thang' and come out with the goods."

The cash and the thought sounds real good, especially to the fact that I ain't got no cash on me now. It's been years since I had that amount of cash on me. Maybe then I can get me a woman and have some fun. I'm not gon' miss this chance. "Say man, its good. I'm in. Just make sure that's all I gotta' do is drive and watch."

"Cool. I'm honored that you wit' us again. I still admire you Joe, man. The fella's will be honored to have you back too. Can you meet me down by the projects on the same ol' stoppin' ground?"

"I'm there. What time?"

"1 am straight up."

"Cool." I hung my cell up as quick as it rang.

03

The crowd is cluttered around my Benz like it used to be years ago. I see nothin's changed. This' the usual on the strip, right in front of the projects. Chew Baby caught my eye as he stepped out from among the crowd and waved me down. I stopped to keep from hittin' em'. I let my window down to get instructions which feels funny cause' I'm used to givin' em'. The cash is much more important than my ego.

"What up Joe, follow me to the end of the corner and pull in the dark alley. I got bout' four wit' me. We'll jump in, you drive, we go in this mansion and do our business, and come out with the goods. You get paid, we all get paid."

Somethin' bout' this don't feel right but all I can think about is the cash that I don't have that I need. I always heard that money don't mean everything but in this case it does. "Arite Chew Baby."

I drove down to end of the corner and pulled in the foggy dark alley just like Chew Baby instructed. I still say somethin' bout' this don't feel right. Chew Baby has a get-a-way van waitin'. I jumped in befo' they did. After about 15-minutes, Chew Baby and his crew jumped in quick with all their masks and dark gear on ready to do business. He introduced everybody as if I already knew em'. He handed me a fully loaded semi-automatic pistol as we pulled off goin' to the destination.

ରୁ

As we slowly approached the huge two-story, circular, stoned driveway of a mansion from about 20 yards away, a sick feelin' has just come over me. Chew Baby and his crew quickly jumped out and ran into the foggy night towards the mansion out of my view. I never moved the van scared it was gon' distract.

Shots suddenly filled the night's air, comin' from the mansion. I'm thinkin' should I take off or go in and see if help is needed? I got out the car, duckin' to shots still filling the air inside of the mansion. I jumped the burgular bared gate and ran around the back, went in from the back, and into the kitchen only to find the worst sight ever. Chew Baby and all of his crew was no where to be found. Glass, blood, and powder from cocaine is all over the kitchen floor and counters. What looks like a thin 125 pound Hispanic man laid by the refrigerator in a pool of blood and a shot gun layin' by his side. Still no sign of Chew Baby and his crew. I'm too scared to call em'. The questioned thoughts of I wonder if they're dead rang in my head? Shots rang out again upstairs and towards me. I shot back to nowhere as darkness cluttered my eye sight. I took cover. I shot into the other room again hearing a yelling woman's scream as if I got em'. I slowly scooted on my knees further only to find a black, familiar woman layin' on the other side of the island with her head also most blown off. My sick feelin' was right. I can pass out. I grabbed her and tried to cover her wounds as my loud cries didn't care if I got caught.

"Wake up! Wake up! I'm sorry! I didn't know you was up in here! Wake up! Don't leave me! Wake up Brenda!..." Police sirons rang outside the house and from the distance as time ran out and they cornered me with the crime as I blacked out.

Sweat's pourin' from my timple like defrost from a melted iced glass. Chains are binding my arms and legs daring me to make a break for it. My time ran out with freedom. Didn't ever think I'd ever get caught. I'll never forget how I felt that night. Seein' Brenda's face, I'll never forget. They charged me with the crime for everybody— Brenda, thin fat ol' Hispanic man in the kitchen, all the dudes in the car that night, accept Chew Baby. He got away somehow. He was never found. Think I was set up. They always wanted the big man to fall. It worked. Now I got life with no chance of parole to figure out how I'm gon' survive up in this hell hole called the Pen. The attorney I had was junk. Probably took one look at my wrap sheet and gave up before the trial ever began.

❧

The jail bars slammed shut to a life lost. Mr. Tough Guy has completely left the scene. The word Thug ain't even on my mind. All my years of bein' in the game and all the lives I took to a bloody hand, I ain't never got caught. Had plenty of jail time but no Pen time. I slipped. Or should I say, I got, got. Chew Baby was slick. He knew what he was doin'. That fool ain't never had no intentions of payin' me my money. Just intentions of settin' me up to fail.

Somebody just had the nerve to flick a blade through my cell bars—straight toward my head. I ducked and connected with the first thought as to why they threw it in the first place. Cuttin' my throat would be an option if I didn't have a slight will to live. It don't take a rocket scientist to know what they wanted me to do.

All the cells closed at the same time to the shouts, "Lights out ladies!" Everybodies runnin' in their cell like their lives depend on it. I guess that means we in for the night. One good thang bout' it is the fact that I ain't got no cell-mate so I ain't gotta' whip no butt.

അ

The heat out here ain't carrin' if me and the rest of the inmates don't like it. If I complain, it gets hotter. If I don't complain it gets hotter. Crazy. The guard won't let up with his stares. I know he waitin' on me to make a break for it. I hate I got the worse job—dirt diggin'. I call it dirt diggin' cause' they got us diggin' dirt lookin' for nothin'. Trees everywhere. Kinda' like a forest all around us with one dirt road in and one dirt road out. Bobwire of the 30 foot fence stops my thoughts from runnin' wild, like breakin' out this hell hole. The devil himself lives up in here. Everybody watchin' and waitin' to cut each other. We ain't diggin' nothin'. Just movin' dirt to another place.

A husky, deep throat voice interrupted my thoughts. "Yo' woman, give me that rake you got!"

He's a fat, 5-foot, stubby midget, Japanese man who got the nerve to step up to me out of no where and call me a woman.

I stood up with dirt and a few weeds in one hand and a rake in the other. "Yo' man you better step back. I ain't nobody to step too."

"You got what I want and I'm gon' get it."

"I ain't got nothin' for you. You gon' get somethin' that you ain't expectin' if you don't step off me. I ain't cho' woman."

"Yea' well, we'll see."

He walked off, snatched his rake that was layin' bout' 5-feet away, and started raking again like he ain't never tried to step to me. I got a feelin' this dude crazy in the head and is waitin' on a chance to steel off on somebody. Somebody must've called him fat and stupid earlier. He looks like the kind that chopped a hand full of men's heads off for laughin' at em' and his weight.

I made the mistake and took my eyes off of him not even a second and he swung the pick of the rake into my right arm, bringin' me down on one knee. The pick's stickin' in my arm so close to my wrist that it looks like my hand's been dismantled. Excrusiating pain just went from my hand to my brain. I grabbed my right arm with my left and tried to swing back with the left but he got a step ahead of me and swung the rake again and popped me in the eye, blurying my vision. I swung in the air hopin' that I would connect, but this dude knows Karati, kick boxing, and judo all in one. I ain't no challenge to him. I've lost before I had a chance to begin. Tryin' to see where I disrespected him. Or am I the chosen one. This dude just hit me with a rake, my brain said. It ain't registered yet that this dude just darn near cut off my hand. Guards are everywhere. Shot guns are raised as one took me down as if I'm guilty. A ray of shots filled the air as I tried to resist and grabbed the guard's gun, shot him, but still lost the battle to a gun shot in my right side. I guess the vision I had came to reality with me shootin' somebody and they turnin' around and shootin' me. The huge dark hole ain't came yet though. No site of fat so. My mind ain't on him noway. All I can think about right now is med's and quick relief. I blacked out.

CB

A bright light beamed down in my eye balls like the sun on the hottest day. Feel like I been dead all my life and just woke up.

Things are blurry and so is the voice I'm hearin', "My name is Susanna. I'm your rehab therapist." Her pretty smile is in focus but nothin' else is.

"Who?" I tried raisin' up. "Where am I?"

156

She grabbed my shoulders and pushed me back down. "Now, now just relax. You're ganna' be fine."

"Woman, where am I?"

Reaching for my clothes is impossible. Prison guards are in the front of me and on the side of me watchin' my every move. I feel the hand cuffs on my left wrist, but I don't feel em' on my right. "Yo woman, what's wrong with my right arm, I can't feel it?"

"I'm sorry to tell you Joe, but you lost your right arm to injury in the fight you had. You were also shot by the prison guards nine times, but miraculously you survived."

"What?!" I had to yell. The fuzz raised up ready to get wit' me. "What're you tellin' me woman?!"

"What I'm telling you is, well, you lost your right arm but we were able to stop the bleeding to your nine gun shot wounds. You lost too much blood and infection built up in your right arm and we had to amputate it up to your elbow."

I'm shocked. How could I be still here? How can all this happen to me? Pricalla's words just popped in my head, *"Joe you better choose God or you won't be here long! That gangsta'-fied, thugish fire you playin' with ain't gon' last long! And when your back is truly up against the wall, either you gon' run to the Lord or you gon' run to the devil. You think you the man with all that pride and can't nothing and nobody beat you, and ain't nobody stronger than you, I'm here to tell you Joe it will all come crashin' down!"* I guess she got her wish where ever she is. The thoughts made me sad and check reality.

☳

I yelled as loud as I could get my voice too. "I can't take this no mo'!"

"Just stay calm Joe. You can make it through this. You're doing good." She grabbed my shoulders again which easily pushed me back down on the bed and made me get quiet real quick.

Man this brawd is strong. Probably cause' it look like she weighs bout' 350 or more. Kinda' gotta' musty smell to her, like she ain't bathed in a day or two and don't care what nobody think. Probably ain't never had no man in her life. She all about work and no play. Her long curly hair or wig, full firey red lipstick lips, coal black eye balls with a touch or darkness underneath; and long eye lashes, might can pull a look from another fat man, but that's all. Her fat neck, fat arms, fat legs, and that fat butt throws me way off. I'm not into fat women, they too much for me to handle. She looks like she a body slam a brotha' if he look at another woman. I cut a laugh inside.

"Say why you so patient and nice?" She started rubbin' my shoulders as part of the therapeutic routine, but it don't feel like it though.

"Cause' it's my job." She softly and quietly answered.

"Naw' I ain't buyin' that. I been up in here going on a month and you have fed me, changed my clothes, kept me calm, treated me like a real free man and not a criminal, and ain't no women ever clothed me unless we just got finished…" I squinted my right eye at her to see how she would receive what I'm bout' to say her, "finished takin' care of business." I nodded my head up and down as if to get her to agree.

"I'm not really into that kinda' talk." She stopped rubbin' and I'm a little embarressed. "Joe I'm only doing my job, and that is all."

"Not by your touch." I said. I tried movin' my amplitated arm back and forth to the daily routine of therapy.

Her beautiful smile blushed a little—makin' her dark complection a dark red color. "Whata' you mean?" She started helping me move my fake arm back and forth, up and down, and then let me do it by myself. A little twinkle sprouted up in her eye balls.

Can't no big woman like me. No! But I'm kinda' likin' her for some reason. Maybe it's her kind soft words? Her touch is unbearable. Probably cause' I ain't had no woman in ages and sensitive to any woman's touch. "I mean, I think you like me."

"I'll be back."

"Where you goin'?"

"I need a break."

"Hope I didn't offend you?"

She walked out sayin' nothin'. Man, I should've kept my mouth closed. This lady ain't been nothin' but nice to me and I don't wanna' loose her to some mean big white ol' lady touchin' me. Probably gone and ain't comin' back.

◌

I woke up to the TV watchin' me. All I can think about is Savanna. I know she gone. Man, I gotta' work on my mouth. I know she don't like me, I was just messin' with her mind. I like to play games with women's minds if I can. I like to see if they weak. I learned this from the streets. You gotta' play with the mind in order to keep from gettin' got. It's a hard pill to swallow, but it's true.

Big women and me don't mix, but this one's different. I feel bad about all the negative things I thought about her. She's nothin' like those fine chicks I messed with in the past. Pricilla ain't even got nothin' on her accept looks and a fine body. But this woman is helpin' me to see life and love in a whole new perspective. I shouldn't be tryin' to get with what's on the outside, it's all about what's on the inside that matters. Never thought this day would come. My whole life has changed. Livin' with one arm was never a part of my dreams as a Gee. I pictured my life way beyond this. Thought Pricilla and me would try it again. Thought Darlene might've come with somethin'. Look like all the women gettin' they self together and findin' an Invisible Love. My thoughts are, why they came in my path considering I ain't on their level. Way too religious.

It don't take all that. The Man Upstairs can't do nothin' for nobody but make their life worse than it was before they ever converted over.

The hospital door opened and closed right around the short corner to my bed. "Good morning." She softly smiled like she always do with a plastic bag in both of her hands.

I smile too. "Thought chu' gave up on me?"

"Never." Her smile lit up the room. Made me forget how heavy she is.

"I likes that. Feels like I can count on you."

"Haven't I proven that?"

"Yep."

"Look I brought some good news. Here's a prosthetic arm for you. We here at Norewood Hospital designed it to fit your arm especially for you. Because your conduct has been exceptional, we wanted to award you with this. We normally do not give this to convicts."

Man, I hate the word convict. But it seems so personal with her, like I'm a free man. "Wow. I don't deserve this. This gon' help me get around better?" We both gripped it and pushed it onto my right, half arm.

"Perfectly better. You won't even know it's a fake arm."

"What can I say? How do I use it?"

"Here, I'll show you."

Ch. 14

New Years come and go. Some of the fella's celebrate in their own way. Some got an imaginary woman to celebrate with. They yell like she winnin'. I here em' all night whinnin' like a dog in heat. They make me wish I had either a dog with me or a brawd that ain't hard at given it up. This is also a time when I wish I had've gotten' to know my people. I know they would come to see me and put some funds on my books.

My cell bars slowly opened to a guard shoutin', "You gotta' visitor! Let's go Quick!"

I jumped up barely able to stand up. Been up in here 5 years and ain't nobody thought of a Gee yet. I guess my wish came true.

☙

"I've come to see if I can appeal your case. You've never been put in the Pen before, and I think I can get you off only if you tell who your sources are."

"Look man, I ain't got no time to be played with."

"I'm trying to help you Joe Quick. But if you don't want my help I can move on to my next case."

He tried walkin' away and the words 'LIFE' flashed before my eyes, which made me re-think his words. "How you gon' get me out of here?" I yelled at em'.

He turned around quick. "I thought you'd change your mind." He came back and sat down and grabbed some papers out of his brief case and handed one to me. "Appeal." I looked at him like, man you better be right. "I can get you a shorter sentence and have you right out of here. Your record is horrible but not horrible for a life sentence. We can get you oughta' here on good behavior and if you give additional information they need..."

"Look man I ain't snitchin'."

℅

Fresh air ain't the same as it was 5 years ago. The real world ain't nothin' like the caged world up in there with real criminals who ain't got nothin' to live for. They ready to take yo' life without a continuous of, I'm sorry. Man, why that lawyer didn't come through sooner than 5 years? I'm askin' myself that everyday.

I lost everything. My Benz. Everything. My Benz was the first thang' they took. That was my pride and joy. Thought I was a bad Gee with the words "Quick" specially made on my front plates. Don't know where it is now. Probably in somebody's junk yard or on somebody's car in different pieces. I'm out to nowhere. I ain't got nowhere to go. I'm homeless and broke. Glad they gave me back my cell after tryin' to use it for evidence but couldn't cause' there wasn't none. Still got all my numbers. I took one step at a time as I looked up and down at the slip of paper with the name, "Restored Life Halfway House" on it. I never would've chose this site if they hadn't of.

❧

This nasty room got the nerve to be freezin' and full of roaches—big and small. My cell blew up.

"Hey partner. You haven't forgotten about me have ya'? I've been trying for years off and on to call you."

I fired up a fresh cigar from the corner store across the busy NY street. Had to add a lil' bit of weed to it, to spice it up. I can't believe it. I want me a woman and the nerd from hell heard my thoughts instead. Why he couldn't be no woman? That's messed up. Pricilla would've been a perfect choice had she not turned a God lover. "What up Chief? Thought you got turned out?"

"Yep turned out to be a call man. I can't count the women I got. Sometimes I dance all night for them too."

I wanna' laugh. All I can think about is his nerdy skin-n-bones naked body dancin' around a stripper pole in front of all those fine women. Crazy. Just crazy. I can't stop laughin'. Man this was a good guy. Now I feel bad cause' I led a good nerdy guy to a bad life. "What chu' mean man?" I asked, already knowin' what he's about to say.

"Yep, I dance. I dance at different places. One of my women is some nice girl name, Candy. She mentioned your name a few times but nothing ever went anywhere because I couldn't find ya' Big Guy. Plus she's mine and I didn't want to share her."

Anger's tryin' to rise up in me, but I can't get mad. I had it comin'. "What did she say bout' me?"

"O' she was just wondering if I still hung out with you and all."

"That's it?"

"Well partner, she's all mine. I paid good money to get her and there was no extra conversation after she laid eyes on me." He had the nerve to sound out a Cheshire Cat cheese, I'm sho' he showin' all thirty two of his yellow teeth. See he still ain't changed.

"It's all good dude, gon' and have yo' fun." We laughed together as if to imagine it. His real and my foney pissed off laugh sounded the air.

THE AFTER AFFECTS

Hey reader, you ain't read the last to Joe Quick. There is a sequel to this novel. You gotta' purchase, "Diamond in the Rough" to see the after effects of Joe Quick's life. Remember, you're still on a roller coaster ride, really it's just begun. Wait til' you see what happens next. Don't expect the end; you'll never be able to figure it out, so read the sequel. You'll be glad you did.........Until then, I'll be waitin' on you in the "Diamond in the Rough". Peace.

THE LIFE CHANGER EXPERIENCE

I have to ask, are you right with the Lord? If not, I don't wanna' wait til' you get the sequel, "Diamond in the Rough" to give you a chance to change yo' life to a better, wholesome, freedom filled lifestyle.

If you know your life ain't what it needs to be and you're ready get it together, repeat after me:

> *Lord I know you are real. My life is not what it needs to be and I'm ready to change it. You said in Romans 10:9 that if I CONFESS with my mouth and BELIEVE in my heart that You were raised from the dead, I shall be saved and my life will never be the same. So I CONFESS that you are Lord and Redeemer and you died just for my sins. Take control of everything and everybody that is in my life. Use me for your purpose in Jesus Name, Amen.*

By repeating, confessing, and believing the paragraph above, you have just become a child of God and your life will never be the same. May God bless you as you find a church home if you don't already have one and get active in the church and allow God to use your spiritual gifts for His glory.

My Song of Solomon

"Many waters cannot quench love, neither can floods drown it…"

These were the words that Solomon Pierre' spoke softly to Barina Grant. She was petite with long kinky beautiful colored hair and had smooth light cream colored skin. While Solomon on the other hand, a poet with words and a spiritual love song in his heart; who had a deep and intriguing voice, a 6' foot stature, honey nut colored skin and muscles to be noticed. His words were ineffable. They were incapable of being expressed into words—they were just that breath taking. The thought of her ever finding true love was almost impossible as she became a 14-year old mother, and went from being homeless to a warehouse worker, to a prosperous writer. After meeting Solomon her feelings turned to him possibly being her eternal love. But through time and wrong choices, she nearly lost her life, her dreams, her career, and almost lost her mind. Yes will be the story that Barina will tell in this hope-filled, dynamic, moving, and purpose filled fiction story of feigned love, later turned into destined divine love…

My Song of Solomon *Prayer Journal*

My Song of Solomon *Prayer Journal*

$10.00 *plus S&H*

A prayer journal

To order, or order in bulk visit Heavenly Realm website.
or write to: info@stephaniefranklinministries.com

Heavenly Realm Publishing
16760 Hedgecroft Dr., Suite 614
Houston, Texas 77060
Toll free: 1-877-599-3237, EXT. 1
heavenlyrealm@heavenlyrealmpublishing.com
www.heavenlyrealmpublishing.com

Position Your Faith for Great Success *Workboo*

Position Your Faith for Great Success *Workbook*

$17.00 *plus S&H*

A Workbook

Position Your Faith for Great Success Workbook is packed with challenging questions from the book, "Position Your Faith for Great Success". It is also filled with a 7-day series of study, bible quizzes, faith scriptures, declarations, confirmations, and answers on faith, success, purpose, and promise.

This workbook will move you to reach for great success and learn how to have faith on how to move the heart of God even though you cannot see how your situation is going to work out.

Remember, it doesn't matter what mistakes you've made in the past, how you've been hurt, how you was not supported, not having the confidence to know that you can obtain great success, or maybe you just didn't know that you had a purpose to fulfill in this life. What ever your situation is, you can still have great success and know that you have the faith and the power to reach the unreachable, to do the impossible, out think the unthinkable, and see what has never been seen before. It's yours, go after it!

You're encouraged to purchase the book, "Position Your Faith for Great Success in order to successfully complete this workbook.

To Reorder Books or request book signings, speaking engagements, and/or workshops and/or seminars, email or visit Website(s):

Stephanie Franklin Ministries
info@stephaniefranklinministries.com
www.stephaniefranklinministries.com
www.heavenlyrealmpublishing.com

BOOKS BY STEPHANIE:

1. When Ramona Got Her Groove Back from God
2. My Song of Solomon
3. My Song of Solomon *Prayer Journal*
4. Position Your Faith for Great Success
5. Position Your Faith for Great Success *Workbook*
6. The Purpose Chaser: For Children Ages 5 to 12
7. God Loves Thugs Too!

The Purpose Chaser: For Children, ages 5 to 12

The Purpose Chaser: For Children, ages 5 to 12

$10.00 *plus S&H*

To order, order in bulk, email info@stephaniefranklinministries.com

Or call: 1877-599-3237

The Purpose Chaser is for the girl or boy that is in pursuit of their purpose in life. You literally have this, "get out of my way" attitude. You want anything and anybody to get out of your way that is not going in the same direction as your purpose and destiny is going. You should have this attitude. In fact, it should be to the point that if a negative person comes in your presence, literally walk away as you let them know by saying, "I'm not trying to hear negativity of any kind from you, I'm chasing after my purpose". When chasing after your purpose, * your mind is on winning, * your goal is to make good grades, * you're attitude is positive, * your eyes are on God and your future. I want you to know that you are a PURPOSE CHASER! You are not too young to chase after your dreams. You are not too young to be what you have always wanted to be in life. You are not too young to make straight A's in school. You are not too young to get an "E" for excellent in conduct. You are not too young to love God. You are not too young to know how much God really loves you. You are not too young to be used by God. You are not too young to be healed from anything and anyone who has hurt you. God loves you and He wants the best for you. Never give up. Stay in school. Listen to your teacher. Learn, listen, and obey your parents. If you are not being raised by your parents, then listen to the one who is caring for you. Obey your leaders. God loves when children love, listen, and obey those who are older than you are. Inside of this book you will find a whole lot of fun stuff just for you to do. You will learn that you are not too young to know your purpose and chase after it. You will also have the opportunity to learn the bible and have fun doing it. You will learn that you were born to win and that God has so many great things in store for you. You will also learn that God loves you and wants you to be the best person that you can be to yourself, to your parents, to others who hang around you, and to the whole world. Do you agree? Great! Let's get started. I'm excited! Open the book, let's go!

Join Today!

Become A Purpose Chaser!

When you join the Purpose Chasers through Stephanie Franklin Ministries, you are saying that "I'm going to chase after my purpose and dreams no matter what. I am going to chase after God with all I have no matter what nobody says. I'm going to chase with a good attitude, I am going to chase in my home, in my community, in my school, in my church; all over the world".

JOIN TODAY! VISIT:

www.stephaniefranklinministries.com

Order Your,
"I'M A Purpose Chaser"
T-Shirt today!

VISIT MY WEBSITE TO ORDER:

www.stephaniefranklinministries.com

Or send email for accurate size and price:

info@stephaniefranklinministries.com

About the Author

Stephanie Franklin's the author of, "When Ramona Got Her Groove Back from God, My Song of Solomon, My Song of Solomon *Prayer Journal,* Position Your Faith for Great Success, Position Your Faith for Great Success *Workbook*, and The Purpose Chaser: For Children Ages 5 to 12". Stephanie is letting her multi-talents shine, but within all of these talents, she's quick to give God all the glory. She is an author, playwright, director, producer, poet, designer, illustrator, motivational speaker, minister, entrepreneur, and educator. Stephanie is all of these things and more. She speaks to the hearts of many who are in need of a life transformation and an up-lifting spiritual and mental move.

Her novels have so many twists and turns that will keep you on the edge of your seat and your eyes flowing through every line. Her spiritual realism, dazzling—heart turning and soul moving novels will make you want to change your life at a heartbeat. Her books of faith, success, and purpose will turn your faith and determination towards a whole new dimension of, "if you just have faith and confidence in yourself, you can do the impossible". Her work ministers to the hearts of millions all over the world, inspiring them to change, and challenging them to love and to live a new and wholesome life.

www.ingramcontent.com/pod-product-compliance
Lightning Source LLC
Chambersburg PA
CBHW071202260626
47162CB00003B/1143